A House

By

G. Voyten

This book is a work of fiction. Places, events, and situations in this story are purely fictional. Any resemblance to actual persons, living or dead, is coincidental.

© 2002 by G. Voyten. All rights reserved.

No part of this book may be reproduced, stored in a retrieval system, or transmitted by any means, electronic, mechanical, photocopying, recording, or otherwise, without written permission from the author.

ISBN: 1-4033-4693-3 (e-book)
ISBN: 1-4033-4694-1 (Paperback)

Library of Congress Control Number: 2002092821

This book is printed on acid free paper.

Printed in the United States of America
Bloomington, IN

1stBooks — rev. 01/07/03

Chapter 1
The House

*T*here was something frightening about the old house on the hilltop in Jefferson Junction. Tucked away on a street that had not seen traffic of any kind for fifty years, hidden behind years of overgrowth, carefully concealed beneath ages worth of decay and neglect, the white sentinel mansion stared as a silent beacon of history in a distorted, tangled mix of thickets and briars. It was known as McNome Mansion in its day, although now the villagers only referred to it as "that wreck of a house where all those people died." Well over a century old and in remarkably good shape, considering the lack of human attention for so many years, the style and grace of its original design spoke of a gentler time spent with residents having class and wealth. In spite of the condition and elegance of the structure, the townspeople were quick to admit nobody ever had the nerve to challenge the reputation of the old residence. If a stranger to town attempted to prove the home was not possessed by overnighting in it, the justification apparently left sometime during one totally horrifying experience within the confines of the structure.

The locals refused to get any closer to the property than the eight-foot tall walls topped with rusting iron spikes and embedded broken glass pieces that encircled the estate. Close enough, they assured me upon my arrival, to still hear the shrieks from within the walls and see the lights winding through the structure at night when some poor unfortunate soul might chance walking by the grounds. The elders of the village, children when the murders allegedly took place within the confines of the mansion, only remembered vaguely that three souls were set free from their earthly bonds while an insane assailant rampaged over them. Two of the bodies were found in bits and pieces surrounding the outskirts of the estate. Some pieces were never accounted for, so the story went. And, according to the local legend, three souls were still roaming the grounds of the estate searching for the missing body pieces and the perpetrator of the crime. Three deaths that literally destroyed the last known members of the McNome family.

    Stories. Legends. Tales. I knew from years of informal investigation that seldom, if ever, were things to happen in a structure rumored to be haunted that could not be justified to physical, living reasons. Am I implying most hauntings are actually explainable by some other means? Yes, in fact, I am saying just that. The reasons for such activities escapes reasonable explanation in most cases but, just the same, I could not argue the conclusive fact that seldom, if ever, was there not identified an earthly tie to a spiritual encounter. And that, I boasted, was why I was interested in dealing with that structure. If the mansion was haunted I would, indeed, be more than willing to assure the townsfolk their stories and legends were still credible explanations. I assured them I would love to be wrong about the tales of the mansion being haunted being true. And, to attempt further authenticating the possibility of a spiritual involvement in the mansion, I brought along my special, psychic companion and friend, Adam.

I had become involved with the McNome mansion and its tales of haunting through a letter I received at work. The letter, from the mayor's office of the town, was at the request of an old, established legal firm—the same firm that had represented the family while they were living and continued to act as executors to the assets and grounds. The conditions stated in the request said only an investigation by me and my company would be allowed upon the property at the request of the legal executors who had researched me and my psychic dealings before having the letter sent. It was there, at the town hall, our investigation began.

In case you have not concluded by this time I will confirm your suspicions about me. Yes, I am an amateur psychic investigator: a "ghost hunter." Although I own and manage a large conglomerate corporation in which I earn more than a modest living, my hobby is what keeps the color in my face and the spring in my step. I do follow other adventures, of course, but investigating reports of ghosts and mysterious happenings sends sparks of excitement through every thread of my being. Of course, teaming up with Adam was sheer brilliance—and fortune. Finding one of his obvious talents is rare indeed. Repeatedly hearing from those seeing him in action that he reveals details long forgotten or only later rediscovered simply confirms how fortunate I was in meeting him in the first place.

Adam and I shared many experiences in places sworn to be haunted and, although Adam had frequently detected the presence of "life forces" in the structures we had investigated as being haunted, never in all his previous experiences had he felt the spirit world had significantly impacted on the environment. He could detect the presence of past events but always felt these were only left over energies and not active spiritual intervention. He could not understand how he could so vividly experience the happenings of the past but understand all the same that he was detecting what he thought of as "recorded events," not active interaction. Somehow, he always assured me, he would know when there was such a thing as a ghost because he felt this ghost would be able to carry on a conversation or interaction with him and others based on what was currently happening at the time. Somehow, I felt this house might give him the opportunity to prove his theories.

The morning of the day we were supposed to begin our investigation we met the mayor and the town council for a meeting concerning the McNome house and the family. The mayor was gracious enough to bring out albums and newspaper clippings from the period of the family's existence and took great care to properly explain the entire history of the event.

"The entire incident took place sixty years ago so there aren't very many left in the town that have a first hand knowledge of the facts," he began. "And evidence wasn't handled like it is today, of course. Methods we now call forensics were in their infancy at that time. It was fortunate, indeed, if they could take body pieces and identify the corpse they came from."

He turned the pages of the book of newspaper headlines, page after page of articles surrounding the

A House

single topic. From what I could see as he hastily turned the pages only two of the bodies were found and, at that, only pieces of them. It appeared the police of the day were readily able to identify the sites of the deaths of the parents by the heavy bloodstains remaining behind that no attempt had been made to conceal but, beyond that, most of the crime remained an unknown. The killer was never found. Worse than that, there was never even a suspect! Yes, the family had employed a small staff to manage the house but, due to a planned two month trip, all evidence of the murders was estimated to be two months old before even being discovered by the returning help!

We sat in the council chambers and the group became silent. I asked casually what the individual members there thought of the present situation and the possibility of the house being haunted.

The mayor spoke first. "I think we are all in agreement. There is something unnatural about that house. Even I have seen the lights within it and heard the screams in the early hours of the morning."

"What about the possibility of kids keeping the effect alive?" I asked.

With a look of complete disbelief the council president was quick to ask, "For years? This has been going on exactly as before ever since I can remember, even as a young child! Do you think we've raised multiple generations of youngsters that get satisfaction getting up at all hours of the night—every night—to carry on this hoax?" He shook his head and smirked. "No, our children will not even venture down the street where that house stands. And, when I was a child, we would not venture down that street, either."

"Just what exactly happens down there?" I continued.

Another councilman spoke. "Two times a night, once at two and once at four, screams and hollers echo out of that old house. If you are foolish enough to be passing by on the street and happen to be looking up at the house, such as I have done, you would see lights passing through the house around those times. The lights look like candles but burn much too white to be open flames."

Another councilman volunteered, "Sometimes you can hear angry voices, sometimes male and female, sometimes two different males. You can hear things banging around inside the house like there is a great fight going on."

A lone councilwoman at the far end of the great table quietly added, "And the one time, when I was a child and dared by my friends to pass by the house early in the morning, about six, I heard nothing but saw a light high in a window next to the right tower, near the third floor. The light brightened and faded for nearly half an hour before the dawn broke and the light faded away." She looked at me like the hands of death had touched her face. "It was something I would never do again."

I continued. "You say some interested individuals have attempted staying the night in the house. Is that correct?"

The mayor answered. "Yes. But every one of them has left the house screaming insanely by two in the morning. Each one I have been exposed to over the years has repeated the exact same story. Feelings of uncontrollable terror have entered them from a

A House

combination of events including hearing voices whispering to them, feeling cold hands running over their bodies, being held down by unseen forces, and, on a few occasions, being physically thrown through the air many feet." The mayor looked dead into my eyes. "Those stories, if told by only one individual, might be thrown out as imagination. But I have been the mayor in this town now for the last twenty years and have had at least ten such individuals stay in that house and each, to a man, has repeated the exact same story although no two were from this town or had ever met each other before their encounters with the house."

I looked at my companion who had remained silent through all the preliminary questioning. I exhaled loudly and said, "Adam, I think we've got something major here."

I continued the questioning. "Who would be the major suspect in the murders, if there was to be made a guess at this time?"

The council president took the floor. "Our understanding of the situation leads us to believe the McNome family was not exactly well loved by the majority of the townspeople. The primary reason, as close as we can figure, was because the McNome's were so much wealthier than the remainder of the village and the villagers resented it. Mr. McNome was a major employer here in those days and the townsfolk felt he got rich at their expense, although, by standards of the day, he was actually a fairly progressive employer, giving health and insurance benefits to his employees back when such were not included in most working establishments."

The mayor added, "He was Irish and, unlike most of his fellow countrymen, became successful in spite of being mistreated by his fellow citizens. I think that is probably what turned the town against him the most. They treated him poorly and he prospered in spite of them."

The councilwoman interjected, "And don't forget the way he was notorious for bringing in outside help if the townspeople refused to work to his standards." She looked at me. "He had several factories at the time, some around here, some in different states.

"He was one of the first businessmen to employ statistical production methods for comparing workers in different locations. If production here did not meet the averages in his other locations, he threatened to import a better grade of worker or move his factory away from the town."

The mayor concluded, "Since he was the major employer in the town the people despised him. They so wanted him to fail but, because of his obvious strengths in business, it was only they that could fail."

I chuckled. "It sounds like that McNome guy was a pretty shrewd character!"

"Shrewd but kind," the councilwoman answered. "He also had a heart of gold and unending kindness and consideration. If a worker fell on hard times due to health or hardship, McNome would secretly help the family out of the problem. The poor children never hungered or went without clothing or shelter as long as McNome was alive. He secretly gave gifts to the children of many of the workers and granted unscheduled, unexpected holidays at a moment's notice, just because he felt morale occasionally needed a boost."

Another councilman continued, "Even the families that did not work for McNome benefited from his kindness."

The mayor concluded. "But he came to own nearly everything, of course. The bank. The food store. The drugstore. The hardware. You name it, if he didn't own it, he probably owned the loan used to finance it. It was rumored that, if McNome had sold or closed all the properties he controlled at the time the town would have shut down solid as a rock."

"So what we have here is a picture of a family of incredible wealth living in a small town that had mixed feelings about him and his family. On one hand they probably appreciated his generosity, on the other hand they despised his wealth and control over probably every major development and project in the town and possibly in the county."

I looked at Adam. "I guess we can't discount the possibility the police department of the time might not have been too anxious or excited about solving the murders, especially if there was a trust set up to see that things continued the way they had always been."

Looking back at the mayor I asked, "But what's the story on this legal firm that has represented the McNome interests all these years?"

"The firm, personal friends of Mr. McNome most of his life in the township, represented him in all his legal dealings, including writing up contracts and agreements for his firms. Of course, all the original members of the law firm are now deceased, but the agreements written up before McNome's death are still active to this very day."

We were given detailed instructions and maps pertaining to the location of the McNome property and it was suggested that we stop at a local shop in town to hire a guide to the property. Yes, we could go without one but, no, it was not recommended. The house had quite a large layout and it might help, especially in the dark, to have someone who had been in the house before. We agreed, thanked the townspeople for their help, and went to our car to attempt finding the house for the first time.

After my lifelong friend, Adam, and I first observed the McNome mansion for ourselves and confirmed its location and condition we proceeded back to the more inhabited sections of town to attempt hiring a guide for our sanctioned stay within the confines of the estate. In spite of massive resistance and great fear from the majority of the townspeople we spoke with we were fortunate enough to be introduced to a gentleman who appeared as old as the earth itself who, although reticent, agreed to guide and teach us about the mansion. The old man, it was said, had lived in the township all his life and was one of the few remaining townspeople to have actually been alive at the time of the murders. It was rumored he may even have personally known the family and, possibly, been a playmate to the girl that once lived there. It was quickly conceded that those statements were all speculation and none of those saying such would actually confirm the statements one way or the other. Just speculation, we were repeatedly assured.

A House

The old man we were about to employ had the look of death itself. His personality was anything but pleasant and the obvious lack of cooperation he displayed made me wonder what good he would be inside the house. But, after speaking with him only a few minutes, enough details came out that I was convinced he was the one and only person capable of successfully leading us through the structure.

He coughed a heavy, smokers congested cough and wiped his mouth roughly with the back of his hand. "You pay cash? I only work for cash."

I nodded. "Of course, we pay in cash. What is your price?"

His deep-set, weathered eyes looked up at me dully from where he continued to sit. "I want five hundred dollars to stay the night." He chuckled and coughed at the same time and added, "Or as long as you fellas think you can stand it in there."

Adam looked at him with great interest. "You talk like you've done this before."

The old man slowly nodded. "Yeah, I'm the one that always gets stuck taking you scientific fellas into that old wreck." He laughed and coughed again. "But the first time a scream echoes through the house and somebody gets thrown through the air all you fancy city folk go running for the door crying for your mamas!"

I smiled a weak, dry smile. "Have you seen people thrown through the air while in that house?"

He laughed a loud, raspy laugh and tossed his old head back, "You bet I have! I've seen dozens of you city fellas go flying across the floor in that old house!"

Adam asked, "And what else have you seen while in that house?"

The old man would not look directly at us. Looking down at his glass on the table he grunted, "Plenty. I've seen plenty in there."

I chanced asking one last sensitive question. "Have you ever seen ... ghosts in that house?"

Still insisting on looking down at his glass he answered in a barely audible mumble, "I can't say exactly what I've seen in there." He paused. He looked up at me. "But I've seen something. I don't know exactly what it was I saw, but I definitely saw something in that house when two o'clock in the morning came."

Adam tried to squeeze more detail from him. "Something like..."

The man's face turned angry and an inner hatred boiled in his ancient eyes. Raising his voice loud enough to attract attention from the rest of the customers in the restaurant he bellowed, "Just something, I tell ya. I don't pretend to know what it was and I wasn't about to hang around to ask! But it was something ... horrible!"

Adam and I knew it was time to stop asking questions and start making our way to the house. I just nodded my head and handed the man $500. "That's enough detail. If you're still willing to go with us, take the money and we'll be on our way to the house while there's still a few hours of daylight."

Adam added as the old man began to stand. "Do you have to go home to get anything before we head for the house?"

A House

The old man stared deep into his eyes, an expression of contempt etched on his face. He smirked. "I won't need anything. Nobody ever stays long enough for me to need anything special. Why would I think this time would be any different?"

Adam and I both nodded. With that, we headed out the door, thanking the proprietor of the restaurant for introducing us to the guide gentleman and paying his bill as we left.

We headed back for the mansion. I could not help but wonder if the guide gentleman would be capable of making the trip in good health. Old, bent and withered, his every action seemed an effort. His breath wheezed in short puffs with each step he made and he had a raspy cough that occasionally surfaced to accent the difficulty he had just drawing each labored breath. His look was unkempt and his scent was of old age itself. His eyes, well hidden among piles of thick, wrinkled folds of skin and bushy white brows, lacked the luster of youth and but occasionally hinted of a spark of interest in life. His clothing consisted of an ancient plaid wool shirt worn out at the cuffs and elbows with torn pockets and many years worth of embedded crusty dirt packed right into the fabric around the pockets. His dirty brown pants were worn shiny in the knees and seat and the hem of the legs had worn into two pieces of cloth where one had originally been folded under. He spoke very little, if at all, to us and constantly refused to allow his eyes to meet ours. Instead, he generally looked toward the ground or off into the distance with a look like he might rather be anywhere else than with us.

I asked him how he felt about entering the house. It was as though I had driven him to instant anger at the very thought and he bellowed back at me with such volume I thought my ear would be burned. "You boys think this is going to be some kind of game! You still don't think things really happen inside that place! You figure you're going to go in there, walk around a little, play your stupid little baby-pants psycho games and come out and tell these people it's all been just their imaginations!" His dull eyes rolled back into his head as his mouth opened wide to expose his chiseled teeth and sticky tongue bellowing, "<u>HA</u>!" He looked down at us like the devil himself with a look so angry I felt death must have created it. In a low, guttural tone he muttered so faintly we could barely hear it above the sound of the car, "You boys will be lucky to live the night. You've never been stalked by death itself before! Your gizzards will be dancing from the front porch before the first light of dawn breaks through the trees!"

Adam's face was blank and pale, his eyes transfixed on the old man's. I pulled up in front of the house and turned off the car's engine. I muttered just before opening the car door, "A real breath of stale air, isn't he?"

At the mansion the gate to the grounds was rusted shut. Luckily, we had a hack saw in the back of my car which I used to saw through an ancient lock that had not had a key inserted into it for a time long enough to make the lock forget it's original purpose. When the lock fell from the massively corroded iron chain holding the two gates together a rain of rust fell as the gates pushed open with piercing shrieks and bone-

A House

jarring snaps that sent shots of apprehension up my back.

We made our way up the winding drive to the walk that entered the house. By the time we approached the front door the guide had already slowed down his progress at entering the structure as though impending doom held him back. I asked him to tell me if there was something wrong. He just slowly looked up at me, then at the house, and then at Adam. He wiped his dry, cracked lips with the back of his ancient hand and the wispy sound of beard stubble broke the moan of the wind hissing through the surrounding trees. He looked deep into my eyes as he narrowed his own. "Don't you feel it? Can't you hear those voices?"

I listened intently for a few moments before answering. "No, I'm afraid I don't hear anything except the wind." I paused. "I must admit I do feel a little uneasy about this house, but I guess I always feel a bit uneasy at entering an abandoned structure."

I glanced over at Adam and noticed an uncomfortable look on his face. Adam, not only a lifelong friend but also a well known psychic, seemed to be able to sense long before I any unusual energies in structures, although I, too, with exposure, eventually would feel the impressions he was experiencing. And so I asked Adam what he was experiencing. "There is trouble here," he began. "I cannot explain all the impressions I am receiving at this moment because it is as though many voices are all attempting to whisper to me at once and each is insisting the others are lying." He continued to look around the area where we were standing and concluded, "There is death here. There is fear here. There is anger and insane violence. I can hear the victims pleading for their lives and weeping about the hysterical futility of hiding or running from their eventual deaths. I hear maniacal laughing. I see a huge knife blade sweeping through the air and blood rocketing away in the opposite direction." He looked me dead in the eyes. "I can hear someone gurgling on blood, drowning and suffocating on their own blood from a severed throat."

I inhaled deeply and exhaled loudly. "Thank you, Adam, for such comforting remarks!" He shook his head as though waking from a bad dream. He smiled. "Shall we enter?"

I nodded and noticed the guide was as white as paper, still staring at Adam. My looking at him must have spoken for itself because he volunteered a reply. "Your friend's words of what happened in this house is ... spooking me. For a stranger not knowing what has happened to say so much of past things scares me."

I tried to manage a smile as I added, "I understand how you feel. I have worked with Adam many times in the past and still marvel and worry at his ability to detect events that have happened in the history of a place that even eye witnesses could not remember until after he refreshed their memories."

I took one last upward look at the house. It was beautiful in its own right, I confirmed. High stone walls and symmetry with two large towers terminating high above us in lofts, many prominent gables all topped with iron vanes, and elaborate filigree highlighting the small porch entrance which was balance with two stained glass windows and two massive front doors with stained glass leaded panels

A House

within. The sheer mass and symmetry of the structure was very castle like and quite majestic.

We began to cross the ancient wooden porch toward the front door. The floorboards creaked and sagged dangerously as we gingerly stepped over them but managed to sustain our weight and, in an instant, we were at the front doors. The doors, stylish and well made by standards of any age, showed the years of abuse and neglect from assaults by those passing by who threw rocks just to hear the glass shatter. Stones laid about everywhere and, where glass had not existed, scars from impact marred the oaken monoliths. The doors had all brass fixtures including a large doorknocker in the shape of a puma's head with its tongue being the clapper.

Our guide immediately reached for the handle to the door and twisted it. Although it hesitated in turning and we could distinctly hear the sounds of metal against unprotected metal rubbing, at a quarter turn the sounds of the latch lifting could be heard and the massive door began moving aside with great distress and complaint. As the door began moving incredibly slowly our guide released the handle. The door, still loudly complaining and cracking and whining continued on its own at an incredibly slow pace. If I had forgotten the sheer mass of the door and the ability of a massive object expertly hinged to move effortlessly on its own, I would have sworn some unseen force was within the house enticingly slowly moving the door open to bid us a speedy if not apprehensive welcome.

Upon entering the foyer I immediately understood this house had been cut off in mid stride of occupation,

G. Voyten

in a living distress. Every object sat as it had when the last living occupant ceased to live. No attempt had ever been made to do a solitary thing to reorder the house. If a pot of flowers had overturned it remained overturned, the plant long ago withering away to dust with only the reminder of it being the overturned pot and spilled soil. Mail received on the last day of life of the occupants was left exactly where it had been collected and placed on a small silver platter on a dark oak stand just to the right of the door as we entered.

The house spoke softly of wealth and conservative class. The decorating was artistic in the combination of fabrics, patterns, metal and stone. Even through years of dust and dirt subtle patterns could still be seen in the carpets and curtains. Furniture was expensive, well placed, well chosen, and generously sprinkled with high-priced antiques from baroque France. I mused that the furniture was still there in the original positions the owners had last seen it and that, after literally generations of townspeople had grown up and assaulted the outside of the structure, the inside with all its treasures was never touched.

Our attention was drawn directly in front of us at the distant but elegant staircase before us. Hanging some twenty feet above it was a magnificent crystal chandelier. The windows of the surrounding area were such that the entrance always would have brilliant lighting as long as there was daylight and, when there was not, the light from the chandelier and the polish of the white marble columns would magnify and enhance the whole feeling of the area.

I asked about the stories of other investigators spending time in the house. If they had, why, then, was

A House

everything as it was when the murders happened in the house? Our guide replied, his eyes still deep within the folds of mystery but a wry little smile crossing his lips, "Because the others never stayed long enough to disturb anything." He paused and looked around for possible evidence of disturbance but, convinced he saw none, continued, "And if anything HAD been moved 'they' probably would put it back the way it was."

Our guide began describing the general layout of the first floor. To our right was a series of rooms consisting of a rather expansive personal library connecting to a large study and a smaller, cozy den. To our left were greeting and entertaining rooms including a front parlor, a large sitting room, a larger dining room, a kitchen, a pantry, and several other small rooms. Our guide's voice echoed from the stone walls as we slowly walked farther into the interior of the house and as he slowly pointed out the doors leading to the various areas he was describing. I noticed the marble floors left tracks from our feet behind like a map leading our way back to sanity and safety outside. How long, I wondered, would it take before we would be retracing those footprints back the other way to the outside and the known environment of everyday life?

I moved over to one wall and stared at the pattern of the wallpaper there. A faint pattern could still be discerned through the filth and age. Paper white silk with a brocade pattern in gold leaf imprinted upon it, it seemed. I loved the pattern and thought how lovely it would be to have seen it in the height of its lifetime, rather than seeing the carcass of what once had been.

Suddenly the front door slammed soundly shut with such force it echoed throughout the house! For a moment I thought all three of us were about to have serious heart problems! After each sighing a large, thankful breath of relief I laughed and commented about momentarily forgetting how well the doors in these old houses were balanced. "Some builders insisted all doors be negatively balanced to automatically shut themselves if left open!" We all laughed weakly about that concept.

It was at that moment I vaguely noticed some kind of suspicious marking on the back of the front door. There in the distance, a few feet away from us, I thought I'd noticed some strange smeared marking running down the door. Adam then noticed me looking toward the door and we both went back to it for a closer examination.

We both knelt to our knees and carefully analyzed the scar left on the door. A mark that looked like some kind of cut from a knife or other sharp object deeply cut into the door. From that point was a reddish black stain which resembled blood smearing and running down the door over the molding and threshold to the floor where a large red stain and many smaller ones still could be plainly seen even through the thick dust on the marble floor.

Adam's eyes followed the markings from the door down to the floor and, as he stared at the stains in the marble he supported himself against the door, his left hand coming to rest upon the laceration itself. As though suddenly electrically shocked he threw himself away from the door, falling away to his side, a frantic look frozen on his face.

"Adam! What's wrong?" I hollered.

A House

Still staring back at the cut in the door, still frozen in shock, he slowly began picking himself up from the floor, never letting his eyes stray from the hole in the door. "I saw it! I felt it! I saw a man killed right here where we're standing! He was carrying a small book in his hands, dressed in house clothes, terrified nearly out of his mind, and he was screaming back at somebody in the dark something about running to the police and telling them to help him. But it was too late. An assailant caught up with him at this point right here, and pushed a large, medieval weapon at the old man so forcefully that it drove him to the floor and against the door where the weapon continued entirely through his body and pinned him right to the door right where this hole is." Adam was now still staring frantically at the door, his breathing was rapid and shallow like he desperately wanted to run away and knew he couldn't. "The old man screamed a blood-curdling scream as the weapon entered his body. And he laid here for many minutes, slowly bleeding to death, with nobody else around except himself and his killer, each staring into the eyes of the other until the old man's eyes transfixed themselves in death and the killer laughed a maniacal laugh that filled the house." He looked up at me. "The killer knew the murders would never be solved without the book Mr. McNome had carried because nobody else had ever entered the property, Mrs. McNome was already dead, and he knew Karen was hiding somewhere in the house!"

He looked back at the scar on the door. "I can still hear the shrieking and the laughing echoing through the house. The murderer congratulating himself at finally proceeding to get rid of the family that he felt had cursed him for so many years." He then looked away from the door and from the guide and me. "I couldn't make out what curse the family had put upon their murderer yet but it must have been something terrible to drive someone to kill three people so mercilessly."

I then noticed how Adam had been holding his chest, rubbing it over and over like it hurt him. "Adam, is there something wrong with your chest?" I asked.

Without even looking up at me he replied, "I can feel the injury. I can tell you exactly where the victim was stabbed and how it felt laying there bleeding to death. I can even tell you how terrifying it was to turn around and see the face of your assailant just moments before the lance was thrust into your body." He looked up into my eyes. "I was there, for a moment. I touched the door where the blood was and I was really there living that moment in history." He sighed and shook. "And I hope this doesn't happen too often because it's scared me to bits!"

It was then we both noticed a peculiar condition: the area directly above the bloodstains was significantly colder than the surrounding room temperature. We both repeatedly moved our hands in and out of that very small, very isolated condition. The area, barely a foot wide, seemed to stretch from the floor all the way up as high as we could reach. The difference in temperature must have been forty degrees or more. Never before had either of us experienced that phenomenon, although we'd both heard of such a thing in stories about other structures.

"Although this does not prove this structure is haunted, Adam, you must admit it does lend itself strongly to the feeling there is a tremendous energy level in this house."

Adam nodded his head rapidly in agreement, still staring at the spot in space where the cold air could show the vapor in his breath if he put his face there and exhaled.

We cautiously continued our tour through the downstairs rooms of the house and had visited half of it when the guide wanted to take us upstairs and show us the living quarters where we could all take bedrooms and deposit our gear before continuing our tour of the premises. The second level had many bedrooms, all quite large and all beautifully furnished. There was also an upstairs sitting room, a bathroom, and what appeared to be a nursery. We had decided, preliminarily, to each take one bedroom. Adam and I took bedrooms opposite each other across the hallway and our guide took one next to mine—actually the first past the staircase. We were situated about halfway down the hallway between the very end and the master staircase leading downstairs.

I briefly looked around my room as I placed my gear on a chair next to the bed. The room had a gentle look to it, even through all the layers of cobwebs and dust covering every square inch. I couldn't put my finger on it but, somehow, the room felt like I belonged there: like someone, at some time, wanted me to be there. I had the feeling I'd been in the room before in a time when it was in its prime. I didn't feel it had been mine, of course, since the decor seemed to be feminine, but, somehow, it felt like I belonged there, like it should have been shared with someone for whom I cared.

G. Voyten

The furnishings seemed to have a certain woman's touch. Even the pattern in the dirty bedspread was delicate and appeared to once have been pink and white. The room had a chest of drawers, two chairs, a low sitting chest in front of the window, and a large vanity with a high back mirror attached to the top of it.

A chill went down my back when, out of the corner of my eye, I thought I saw a face other than mine being reflected in the dirty mirror atop the vanity. The sight, lasting but an instant, seemed to be that of a blonde girl. Even though I only saw it for an instant I thought it had been looking straight at me and gently, knowingly, smiling at me. But I didn't make too much of it and I soon joined the others in the hallway without mentioning my vision. I felt I was only imagining it based upon the impression it should have been a woman's room and how I longed to understand the empty feeling inside me regarding the room's history.

Our tour continued with us examining each and every room upstairs for signs of life, death, and history. Beneath the layers of heavy dust must lay the clues leading to the solution of the murders, we thought, but where to begin would be a major problem. The one point we all agreed upon was finding the book Adam had seen in the death scene would help solve the puzzle. Find the book, read the clues, and solve the mystery.

We also felt that breaking up would probably allow us to cover more territory than staying together. The guide claimed no visitors had ever stayed one entire night within the confines of the house since the murders had taken place and, just to humor him if nothing else, we had all tentatively agreed we would

A House

be out of the house by morning at the very latest. Adam and I laughed at the thought: solve a sixty-year-old mystery in less than twenty-four hours! He also felt no visitor had ever been bothered by the spirits within the house during the daylight hours, so we felt separating would not endanger us.

As we proceeded up and down the main hallway there was one problem I immediately became aware of: there was no way of getting to the third floor. Two doorways, one at each end of the long hallway, probably led to the third floor. Two doors were, of course, locked. Based on the resistance to budging I guessed the doors were dead bolted from the other side. Strange, I thought, why would both doors be dead-bolted from the other side? Obviously, there must have been additional ways up into the third floor that we just didn't know about and our guide was unaware of or unwilling to discuss. Or, as our guide would try to have us believe, the spirits of the house had bolted the doors from the other side to keep the mystery unsolved.

Chapter 2
The Tower

*W*e agreed to meet downstairs in the library at dusk, about two hours later. We each agreed to gingerly examine the rooms, both upstairs and down, for signs of Mr. McNome's diary or other things which might lend insight into the events that had taken place. We returned to the first floor and broke up to each search alone.

I couldn't explain why, but I had been immediately drawn to a front room next to the library. It appeared to be a small study room. It was dark and felt very close and the air was musty and thick. But some feeling insisted I start my search there and so I did. Had I heard voices? No. Had I any evidence that this was where things would happen? No. But, somehow, I knew there was something coaxing me to that place and, I felt, it had less to do with evidence of the book we were searching for than it did with a way to get to the third floor. My searching, then, was a casual mixture of looking in obvious places for the book and a more intense looking for something much larger: a hidden doorway which might lead out of the room and up a staircase toward the third floor.

The room was strangely misshapen. It was not rectangular as were most rooms in this well-designed home. And then I realized why: I was in a room where

A House

one of the two towers attached on the outside of the house!

I went to the "odd" wall. No, it was not rounded as one might expect it to be if attached to a circular tower. Rather, it was just an angular cut across the room that consumed one square corner with a flat wall. In front of the wall was a roll-top desk and behind the desk as well as the remainder of the adjacent wall was ceiling to floor velvet drapery. I'd originally thought it was only an attempt to sound isolate the room or used as some kind of textural accent feature. However, believing there was something more to the irregular wall than just esthetics, I began pressing my hands into the drapes, trying to feel what features lay behind them.

Directly behind the desk, at the most difficult position to get at, I felt the outline of a door, although flush mounted to the wall with no framework surrounding it. With great difficulty I managed to move the draperies and see that, in fact, there was a doorway.

Before proceeding further I returned briefly to my room and armed myself with a flashlight, a pen and tablet, rubbing paper and crayon, and various other little equipment pieces I had found useful in the past to help establish clues. Turning to leave the room I happened to glance at the vanity mirror and noticed something appeared to be written in the dust on the glass. Looking closer it appeared to read, "EJ must die". I stared at it very closely and a chill ran down my back as a gentle icy wind passed by and, behind me in the reflection from the mirror, I thought the image of a woman had walked by!

I turned around hastily to see who it had been walking so quickly behind me and realized the person would have had to be walking at great speed ... directly across the bed! I examined the floor and the bed but, no, the dust had not been disturbed in either place. Somehow, deep within me, I felt, though, this person was real and trying to get my attention! However, I felt the message on the mirror was probably the attempt of either the guide or one of the villagers who knew we would be attempting to solve the mystery to throw clues at us that would lead us astray from the task at hand.

Still not sure about what was going on, I rushed back downstairs and to the room with the hidden door, still not letting either of my other two team members in on what I was about to do. Foolishly, I guess, I felt I might be scorned for frivolously chasing my tail on hidden passages rather than hunting for clues. No matter, I assured myself, I was compelled to pursue the course.

I found it was easier to lift the drapery and place myself beneath it than it was to find an opening in it to let myself in. Being in such darkness the flashlight allowed me to find the door's release latch easily, even though it was mounted flush with the surface of the door. I would have had great difficulty finding it in the dark without the flashlight.

Strangely, the door opened absolutely silently, never making so much as the slightest noise. On closer examination I discovered the door hinges were not the conventional pin type but, rather, one hinge at the very top and very bottom resting in sealed bearings like

A House

those used in machinery. I entered the tower chamber and closed the door silently behind me.

Although there was a window immediately in front of me that looked out toward the front of the house the tower was still not very light. It had to do with the amount of dust and dirt on the windows. Inside the tower was but one feature: a circular staircase going nowhere but up. And so I began climbing the stairs. My attention was drawn, though, to the pungent smell of the area. Rust, rot, mildew ... death, I thought. The thick air hung with the smell of old age and certain death. There was so much dust in the air it was difficult to breathe without coughing. My eyes soon felt thick with dust. I could taste the filth in the air.

In a short while I came to a landing and a much smaller window than the one on the first floor. On the landing was another door, again, with a latch mechanism relatively flush to the door. I knew it had to be the second floor and I quietly opened the doorway and peeked out.

I was looking into a large bedroom on the second floor at the opposite end of the house from where we had been staying. The room was moderately dim from the curtains being nearly shut but I was curious enough to enter further and examine where I had ended up in this room.

I entered the room completely and looked back at the door I had just passed through, No wonder I hadn't realized before that there was a door! From the bedroom side it was a full length mirror and part of the frame to the mirror was actually a push panel that opened the door!

My impression of the room was that it was not used much by the household. There were no personal effects that would give a room the feel of an individual. The colors, as far as I could tell, were neutral colors that would not offend either a male or female occupant. The paintings on the wall were pastoral and rather impersonal. There were no pictures of individuals. There were no personal effects on the dressers. Just out of curiosity I opened the dresser drawers. Nothing. Not one object. I even used my flashlight to closely examine the corners of the drawers, beneath the drawers, behind mirrors, even under the bed and between the mattresses. Nothing. Nothing contained within the framed pictures or behind them. And then, with a feeling so strong I nearly turned and answered, I was once again beckoned to continue up the stairway to what lay beyond.

I returned to the tower stairway and silently closed the door behind me. Looking up into the tower it seemed to get darker toward the top, even though I thought I remembered there being another window at the very top. Regardless, I thought, I must continue up. So I climbed slowly up to the third floor, the third window the same size as the last, the third door, and the third landing.

I don't know why but I began to feel very uncomfortable about going through this third doorway. I had a feeling of an unexpected encounter with … what? Something, I told myself. Although I hadn't experienced anything to convince myself to the contrary, I felt my experiences might seriously change when I passed through that doorway into whatever laid

A House

behind it on the mysterious third floor: the floor being somehow guarded behind locked doors. I had the terrible feeling that something—evil—was linked to that room, something on the order of death itself. The air felt cold and even more heavily laden with dust and mildew. But the cold seemed to penetrate my clothing unnaturally, giving me great apprehension about proceeding.

In the dim light of that landing I could still make out the latch and pressed it. Again, perfectly silently, the door opened to a room, only this time the room beyond was very, very dark—nearly black. The nearest window to the room was many feet away, one of the gables on the house, and the drapes were closed tightly as though to keep the secrets of the room contained within it.

A very uncomfortable feeling kept drawing me further into the room, even though it was nearly impossible to see where I was going. Somehow I had forgotten completely about the small flashlight tucked away in my pocket. I felt like something or someone was behind me pushing me into the room and I felt myself stepping clumsily in even though I could absolutely not see where I was going. The air was thick and stale and unusually cold and I still felt there was something wrong there—something tragic I could not explain.

Suddenly, without even realizing what had happened, the door behind me closed itself so rapidly I felt the breeze from it as it passed! I distinctly heard it snap latched. Strange, I thought again, the other two doors did not move when opened, one way or another, why should this one? I could feel the goose bumps building all over me and my stomach began to knot up. But before I could wonder much more it happened.

It sounded like a whisper, like someone who wanted to let me know I was not alone without frightening me. It was a whisper I first thought might just be sounds of the house. I could not make out what was being said or if, in fact, I was hearing intelligence or just hissing sounds. Still frightened nearly to death, I chanced whispering back, just in case I was actually hearing the voice of another.

"Is there someone here with me?" I whispered so faintly I could barely hear myself.

The whispering returned, a little louder but still far away. "Yes, I am here." There was an awkward, terrifying pause. "Please do not turn on your lamp or open the drapes yet. I am frightened."

In a louder, hoarse whisper, I answered, "***You're*** frightened! What do you think *I* am?"

The whispering got louder and closer. I thought I detected a female tonality in the voice. "I must talk to you. I must tell you…"

I was still terrified but I tried to adapt to the experience. It had to be someone from the village that got into the house and hid there, waiting for someone to be alone with her so she could tell what she knew without arousing suspicion from the rest of the townsfolk. Based on that assumption, I felt much more comfortable with myself. I spoke in a low voice, not quite a whisper, "Ok, go ahead and tell me what you must say."

The voice grew stronger and closer. I could feel breath on the back of my neck and I knew it had to be someone just as I'd earlier surmised. But, somehow,

A House

there seemed to be something familiar about the voice as though I had spoken with this person before somewhere, sometime. "I need to tell you what happened here. I know you are here to solve the mystery of the murders that happened in this house."

"Yes, I am. And I am also here to find out if the townspeople are correct about the spirits of the dead still actively roaming this house."

I felt this person gently touching both my arms on either side, still behind me. I could feel her face touching the back of my head and her lips moving as she spoke so silently into my ear. "I want to help you. I would like to help you understand what happened here. And I would like you to help end the curse on this house and all those who lived here."

The room seemed to warm. I felt even more comfortable. The woman obviously only wanted the truth to come out. Maybe she felt some kind of obligation to the McNome family. Maybe, somehow, she was actually one of the only remaining McNome heirs who had come back to avenge her family. Maybe she somehow had to clear the name. So I played along with her. "So what would you like to tell me?" I paused a brief moment. "And why me?"

Her voice continued a little louder. "I chose you. I trust you." She paused. "I ... care for YOU."

Now my curiosity was getting the best of me and I attempted to turn around to see who was back there holding me. As I attempted to turn I began saying, "Who are you?"

The hands on the back of my arms changed from lightly touching me to strongly grabbing me and definitely kept me from turning around. The woman's voice, a little louder and much more intense and frightened, exclaimed, "Please don't turn around! I'm still frightened of you and I know I'm not supposed to be here with you ... alone like this!"

I chuckled a little bit to myself and replied, "Don't worry, I won't tell anybody about you and I meeting up here, ok?"

Her grip loosened. "Not even my father?"

I nodded. "Not even your father." I paused. "I'm sure I don't even know who your father is!"

She returned to barely holding on to the back of my arms. "No, no I don't believe you've met my father yet." She paused. "But Father may find out anyway and he has never allowed me to talk to men that he did not know properly first."

Without making an effort to turn around again, I asked, "Why won't you let me look at you? Are you afraid I might recognize who you are and tell someone in the village about it?"

She laughed a little and stroked the back of my arms lightly. "No, you will not recognize me. And there are very few villagers who would recognize me." Her voice had softened. It sounded like she was beginning to enjoy herself.

"Ok, then, how about us sitting down and having a long talk?"

She hesitated in answering. "Well ... only if you promise you will do exactly as I say and do not try to do things that frighten me."

My eyes had finally adapted as much as they could to the dark. I could begin to make out objects within the room. I could clearly see items of furniture and things lying about on the floor. When I finally could

A House

make out a chair very close by I slowly, cautiously moved over to it and sat down, turning around to face back toward where I had previously been standing by the hidden doorway and where the pretty female voice had been coming from. There, still well hidden in the shadows of the room, I could see the shape of the woman who had been speaking with me. No, I could not see much detail, but I could make out, vaguely, some major features.

She was young, probably in her early twenties. She was blonde. She was still standing and she appeared to be wearing a dress. But this dress was a full length dress with puffy shoulders. I could not clearly make out the features of her face but her mannerisms convinced me she had grace and class, unlike the majority of the village people we had seen.

"Are you from here?" I asked.

"Why, yes! I am from here!" She nodded. She held one hand in the other before her about waist-high.

"You seem so unlike the other villagers I met today," I continued.

She giggled a little. "Oh, that's probably because Father would not allow me to mingle with the other villagers. He insisted I be sent away for schooling. That was what people of my station were supposed to do, he told me."

I hesitated. "Am I ... going to be allowed to know your name?"

She laughed a little. "Karen." The sound of her voice was light and airy, kind of like the gentle tinkling sounds of a wind chime.

"Thank you, Karen. And my name is..."

She interrupted. "I know your name. I know many things about you. I know your friend, Adam, and I know much about your guide."

Puzzled now, I asked, "How would you know these things? We only spoke with a very few people in the village and you weren't one of them."

"Just the same," she continued, "I know much about you." She paused. "And that is why I feel I can trust you with my secrets. I probably know more about you than you do about yourself."

I wanted to know more about her and how she influenced me to find the hidden staircase and climb up until I found her. But, before I could even ask, she answered, "I cannot answer all your questions right now. I don't have much time and I can't allow you to be missing from the others for very long. Besides, if my father knew I was here he would be very upset with me and I love him too much to allow that to happen. So let me at least get you started on the right track in your quest for the answer to this mystery."

I interrupted her. "Karen, don't you want to sit down and take your time?"

She laughed a little laugh. "No, I don't have to sit down and I cannot take much time."

Before she could continue I had two more questions I needed answered. "Why do I feel like I know you and why won't you let me see you in the light?"

I could tell by her voice she really wanted to spend more time with me and the tone of her voice was soft and affectionate. "You feel like you know me because our spirits have intermingled in the past and even in the present and we have feelings toward each other.

A House

And I can't let you see me in the light because this is not the time for you to know who I am."

"Feelings toward you. Are you saying that, spiritually, we care about each other but, physically, we have never met before?" I was beginning to think the girl must be some kind of spiritual mysticism fanatic or something.

"You have never met me before physically but we have met—in our dreams. I have shared moments with you while you slept."

Right, I thought to myself. This was a great line I wish I'd thought of! "But…"

She interrupted one last time. "But I am running out of time and so are you. Please … please let me continue. You are my only hope. You are the only one brave enough and understanding enough to solve the curse of this place and set things right within the walls of this house. If you fail, the curse, the very souls of those slain here, will continue to roam restlessly throughout time. The chance for the souls in this house to rest comes only once every ten years on the anniversary of the murders and that date approaches."

She must have seen the look on my face or felt the futility in my heart for she made one more personal comment before continuing. "I think I understand what you are feeling right now. I know I have confused and confounded you and made you feel a part of you is missing. I cannot allow that to interfere with your task." The look in my eyes must have let her know I still didn't understand and I needed more. "I will try to tell you more later. And I will try returning and letting us share each other's company before your task is done." She paused. "And I will try to avoid meeting you in such darkness." Her voice grew a little louder and sterner, although not threatening. "But that is all I can promise for now! So please understand!"

I smiled. "Very well, Karen. I understand. You have something very important to tell me and I should settle for taking care of business first and building relationships second."

I could see her face a little better by then. A smile crossed her lips. I could tell she was very attractive. Her features were fine and I was intrigued to know more about how she really looked. "Thank you for understanding. I know how difficult this must all be. It is for me as well, please believe that."

She sighed one short puff of breath and continued with her story. "Adam has had two paranormal experiences already while in this house, once at the front door where he detected voices all talking at once and a close encounter with the death of one of the family members at the front door."

A shock ran through my body like a needle had been inserted in my spine. How could she know that? In amazement and without taking time to ask, I only nodded my head.

"Adam referred to a diary the slain man had been carrying with him that detailed this individual's involvement with the murders. The impressions of that family member at that time were that the diary held the only detailed account of the murders. That impression was wrong! Another account exists of the murders in another diary which resides within the house."

I interrupted. "But the original diary?"

"Ashes in the fireplace in the library. But there are other items hidden in the house that also lend evidence

A House

against the murderer such as the weapons used in the killings, the stained clothing, the tunnels out of the house to where the pieces of the murdered family members were found."

Her face hardened and her voice, although still just above a whisper, had great tension and anguish in it. "I want to help you find these items and incriminate the man who did these things."

"I don't know how you could possibly know these things, Karen, but I'm willing to give it a try."

She continued, "You will be able to learn who the guilty man is by reading the diary pages held…"

She interrupted herself and her head slightly turned as though listening to something that I could not hear from where I was seated. She continued. "Someone is coming and you must go and rejoin your others right away."

"But what about…"

She began to look worried. "Not now! I will try to meet you again later! I promise!"

She turned toward the hidden door, which I could not really see at all, and the next thing I knew, the door was opening and she was stepping away from the light. "Now please leave immediately! Exit on the second floor bedroom and tell your friends you did not hear them calling for you!" She hesitated for only a moment. "And it would not be a good idea to mention much about this encounter with your two companions. We can trust Adam but there is something familiar about the old man who acts as your guide. There is something suspicious about him. When you all approached the house my father saw the man and became enraged. This man puts you all in great jeopardy."

"And as for me?"

She was becoming impatient. "You will remain safe as long as my family is near to protect you. But please do not trust your guide companion. I cannot be close enough to warn you if he endangers your life."

I immediately rose from the chair and stumbled my way across the room until I was standing right beside her. I was close enough to touch her and I could just barely make out the glistening of her eyes in the darkness. I stared deeply into her eyes ... two beautiful deep blue green eyes set in a soft perfect pink face. Her eyes told me her feelings for me went deeper than she had suggested and pleaded for something more than just a handshake. I don't know what compelled me to act, not being very brave where involvement with women was involved. Without hesitating, I put one arm around her and gently but firmly kissed her on the lips. She tasted sweet and she smelled of powdery perfume. She pulled herself to me by wrapping both arms around me and totally involved herself in the kiss that lingered longer than I had intended. When we separated our faces met cheek to cheek in an embrace. She finally whispered, "I love you ... I've always loved you," as she pushed me through the doorway back into the tower and hastily closed the door behind me.

Without hesitating I knew I must do as she said for fear everything would crumble around me and further contact with her would forever be impossible. I hurried down the stairs as fast as I could while remaining absolutely silent and was quickly at the second floor

A House

landing where I immediately entered the bedroom and instantly closed the tower door behind me. Running through my troubled, confused mind was the surprise I had given myself regarding that girl! Could I believe I had just met a girl and, completely unlike myself, found the courage to kiss her? It was all I could do not to grin and brag about it! Me! Actually finding a girl during an investigation that was drawn "to my spirit!" What a great beginning to a mystery!

At that exact instant Adam and the guide entered the room and nearly scared me to death! "Where have you been, man? We've been looking for you for the last five minutes!" Adam looked at me strangely as soon as he saw me.

I didn't exactly know what to say. It was like being caught with your hand inside the cookie jar. What was I supposed to say? "I thought, what the heck, I might as well find a hidden door to the towers and follow this unexplainable feeling that someone was calling me up to the third floor and then meet this beautiful young woman who actually knows the secrets of this house but, somehow, actually knows us and especially me and, somehow, has the hots for me and we were going really great and got to know each other really well when she knew you were looking for me and forced me to leave even though I really, really didn't want to because I really like her a lot?" Yeah, sure. So I kind of told the truth. "Oh, well, I meandered up here and was investigating this bedroom for clues and I searched it really, really well but I didn't find anything and I was just about to come down and get you when…"

Adam had grabbed both my shoulders and began to turn me toward him, probably to stop me from rambling on, but, the instant he touched me, he looked deep into my eyes and started grinning. In my heart I felt he had to know. And I thought I'd been terrified upstairs when the girl began talking to me in the dark! "I've never seen you like this, Alex," he said, still grinning. "You're in love with her, aren't you!"

If I'd been shocked before it could not possibly have been anything compared to how I was at that very moment. Without further explanation, I meekly answered, "Yes."

The guide asked, "Love?"

I looked deep into Adam's eyes with a look that said, "don't explain it further." I continued, "It's nothing serious. He's just teasing me about a girl I've been dating at home."

Adam drew near, looking closely at my face. He touched the cheek I'd touched against Karen's, then he sniffed close to my face. He whispered, "I wanted to get the full impression of her while the energy left behind was strong. We'll discuss this later." Then, moving back a bit, he said loudly, "I thought I saw a scratch on your cheek but I must have been fooled by the lighting in here."

Adam whispered one more thing before moving away. "I think I felt this energy presence in some other room."

Adam said he wanted to investigate a feeling he was experiencing in a voice loud enough to make it sound like this was just another psychic encounter he had to handle. He led us out of the bedroom and down the hall to another bedroom: the one I had chosen or

A House

thought I had chosen to spend the night in. He slowly made his way over to the dresser and picked up a filth-covered frame from the dresser and tried polishing it off with his hand, then he handed it to me. "Any idea who this is?"

I couldn't believe my eyes. It was <u>her!</u> Those same beautiful big blue green eyes in that soft pink face framed by long light blonde hair. Even the look on her face in the old photograph looked like it was taken with me in mind!

The old man looked at the photograph. "That is Karen McNome, the daughter of Brian McNome, master of this house. She was about twenty four years old when she died."

I was startled! I asked, "Do you mean I have chosen Karen McNome's room to sleep in tonight?"

He looked up at me, "Yes, I suppose you have." He smiled a strange smile. "Does that have any great significance?"

I shook my head and looked down at the old photograph I still held in my hands. Very quietly I answered, "No, no great significance." Adam only smiled.

I put the photograph down after I had thoroughly cleaned it up and could very plainly see Karen's soft, loving face staring back at me. "Now what were you going to tell me before you had this feeling about coming into this room?"

"Oh, we discovered something down in the library I thought you'd better look at."

I started out of the room. "So let's go down and have a look!" I allowed the others to leave ahead of me but I lingered a moment in the room, wondering what was going on and why did I have this uncomfortable, empty feeling aching in my chest. I felt like I had gained and lost something very precious in only mere minutes.

We started down the hall with the guide leading the way. Quietly, with Adam walking beside me, I whispered, "How did you know? How did you know about Karen? And what's going on here?"

Adam kept looking straight ahead and only briefly whispered back, "I can't go into it right here. Wait until the guide is not around. There's more to this old man than we'd thought."

Chapter 3
The Library

*W*e arrived in the library. The room was majestic in its size and excellent construction and design. Massive bookcases lined three walls and, occasionally, there were openings where paintings were mounted. A massive table occupied the entire length of the room surrounded by large, solidly built chairs, each with its own lamp centered on the table. A rolling ladder was mounted on a track that rounded three walls of the room to aid in obtaining volumes out of arms reach and three crystal chandeliers were spaced over the length of the table. There were windows across the entire back of the room looking out across the back of the property through some very large trees close to the house. The windows, still perfectly in tact, did not have drapes over them but were bare and allowed filtered sunlight in through the trees outside.

The old man hobbled over to a large dark spot on the carpet in one corner of the room. Pointing and looking down at it he said, "I think this spot may be blood of one of the members of the family that was killed."

Adam and I got down on our hands and knees and carefully examined the spot beneath the thick layer of sticky dust. And then Adam made the mistake of attempting to wipe the dust away with his hand. When his hand hit the bloodstain he was projected ten feet backward across the room, impacting on a bookcase against one of the walls. He fell to the floor and the noise of the impact echoed throughout the room and house like the report of a rifle. He just sat there, dazed, and I rushed over to help him but, before kneeling to the floor, noticed that, directly above his head where he had landed, was a portrait of a woman, most likely, Mrs. McNome.

"Adam! Adam! Are you all right?" I shouted.

He was semiconscious. The side of his face began showing a red, swelling impression of a complete handprint as though someone had slapped his face incredibly forcefully. As he shook his head he muttered, "That man can really hit!"

"What are you talking about?"

He weakly looked up at me, a small trickle of blood running off the corner of his mouth and from one nostril. "I guess it was the murderer." He looked back at the spot. "Yes, it was the murderer. He had a confrontation with Sarah right here. She was having an argument with him and was about to get her husband to expel Johnson when he caught her off guard and slapped her face so hard she fell all the way over here. She tried to scream. A struggle ensued. Johnson took a hunting knife out of his boot, grabbed her by the hair, and slit her throat without hesitating. Then he stood over her, laughing about how she wasn't going to be able to tell anybody about the money now. He just stood there laughing while she drowned in her own blood."

I helped him up. "Adam, were you listening to what you just said? You said 'Johnson.' You've come up with a name for the murderer! And you've come up

A House

with a motive! You mentioned money, that there was some sort of confrontation about money!"

He looked up at me, his face lighting up like someone had just told him the meaning of life. I helped him to his feet. "Yes! Yes, that's it! Elias Johnson was the handyman around here. He was one of the servants. Several times for about a month before the deaths of the McNome's, money had disappeared from the rooms of certain family members. Mr. McNome even claimed some bonds and negotiables had been misplaced or stolen but, since nothing had ever been taken from the house before and the same staff had served the house for at least the previous ten years, the McNome's naturally assumed it was a personal misplacement, not theft, that caused the disappearances. Sarah discovered Elias had stolen money one day when the safe had not been closed all the way. It was a substantial sum of money for the time, many thousands of dollars. Sarah, in good faith, had asked Elias to return the money. Elias denied he had taken any money. Sarah grabbed his tool kit, Elias grabbed back, the box fell, the money poured out along with the tools and a few pieces of jewelry Sarah recognized as belonging to her. Sarah, again, insisted Elias give back the items. Elias argued that it was his money he had been saving from past jobs. Sarah said her husband would have to settle the matter. Elias made sure she never got the chance to yell for her husband."

We turned toward the guide whose ashen face told all. His eyes stared back in terror. His mouth quivered. His voice broke as he spoke. "Nobody knew that story. <u>Nobody</u>." The look on his face was one of such horror

I was hoping he would not succumb to a heart attack on the spot. He tried to regain his composure. "I don't know if it is true or not. The story in the village only said someone, nobody knew who, murdered the McNome's. A motive was never known."

Adam, gently touching the red mark on his face, asked, "Do you mean the townspeople thought the deaths were just some serial killer who happened through the house and killed all the occupants?"

The guide nodded his head. He answered, his raspy voice returning to what I had to assume was its normal tone. "Yes. You see, because the McNome's were not public people and were not well liked, nobody knew there had been murders in the house. In fact, the coroner of the time stated, based on the level of decomposition of the body parts by the time they were discovered, the deaths could have been months prior to the parts showing up."

I felt that a little unlikely since the family employed a staff of support people. "Come on, how do you expect me to believe the household staff didn't suspect anything? When they got up and didn't find the family around the morning after the murders didn't anyone get a little suspicious?"

The guide chuckled but his eyes were still deathly serious. "I guess it would have been suspicious if the McNome's hadn't planned a two month vacation at that very time. The staff had left the day before the McNome's were supposed to leave for their vacation. The family planned on leaving directly in the morning and having breakfast on the train on their way to their ship to Europe."

A House

I continued. "And so there was nobody in the house except for the murderer and the family at the time of the deaths and nobody returned to the house for two months afterwards?"

He slowly, solemnly nodded his old head. Hoarsely he added, "That's right. When all the support staff returned to the house a day before the family was supposed to return, all that was found was the empty house and the bloody clues to the deaths of Mr. and Mrs. McNome." He hesitated. "The body parts showed up sometime after that time, I was told."

"What ever happened to Elias Johnson?" I asked.

The old man rubbed his bristly beard and slowly shook his head as he looked off into the distance at some unseen vision, a whisper of a cunning smile curling his parched lips. "I can't really say. The family had given the staff two months off while they were supposed to be off in Europe on vacation. That is why the furniture is covered with sheets to this very day. It wasn't like somebody came in here after the deaths and prepared the house to stand empty for eternity. It was like this because the staff left before the murders took place and the police insisted nothing be disturbed in the house. But I suppose Elias Johnson, like the rest of the staff, returned to the house to work." He looked at me with a sneaky, knowing look in his eyes. "It wouldn't have been like Elias was suspected of doing wrong or anything." He coughed a wheezing, congested cough. "I'm sure Elias Johnson returned to work like everybody else!" A sneer crossed his bristly cheeks. "After all, who's to say Elias Johnson actually did this thing you're friend says happened? Your buddy here is just mouthing things he thinks he feels! Who's to say those feelings are right?"

Adam, still rubbing his face, even admitted, "The guide may be right. Even if I am getting psychic energies, there's nothing to say they must be correct. Who can say what happened here?"

But, as I looked at Adam, his eyes were saying, "… But how could a psychic impression of a woman being murdered name an unknown name of someone who could be suspected, since the individual was an actual member of the support staff and two of us in this room had no idea of the names of any of the individuals involved before this event?"

We sat at a long, dark table in the center of the library. Adam's face had finally returned to normal and he'd recovered from the incident. I began to wonder. "What ever happened to Karen McNome?"

"She was never found. No part of her body was discovered. Nobody ever knew whether or not she had actually died." He paused for a moment, again lost in remembering the past. "It was even rumored she may have killed her parents in order to get their money."

"Did she have any other relatives who might have had a claim to the McNome money?" I asked.

"No, as far as I know, she was the last of the McNome's."

Adam asked, "Did money disappear from family bank accounts? Were there ever any reports of Karen being seen anywhere spending the money?"

The old man shook his head and coughed a gut wrenching cough. "No, no there were never any stories about nobody spending a lot of McNome money." He paused. Lowering his voice he added, "But, since

A House

Karen McNome was never seen again, it was always rumored she actually took the money and ran off somewhere to spend it. Maybe even took that trip to Europe she and her family had planned. Why, maybe she lived there the rest of her days spending that money."

I found that hard to believe. "And there were never reports about the handyman spending the money?"

"Nope. Never. If that feller actually killed those people the way your friend here believes then he must have been too scared to spend the money." He paused a few moments. "Or maybe he hid the money in the house somewhere and was too scared to come back for it."

Adam had fully recovered from the incident and we headed for the kitchen to have some dinner. As we walked across the house and from front to back Adam asked, "What ever happened to the handyman?"

Without even looking up as he walked the old man said only, "Nobody knows, nobody remembers..."

As we walked Adam mentioned only one other impression and he whispered it ever so softly directly in my ear: "There is a surviving relative somewhere, I think. Mr. McNome had a lawyer researching where this family lived before the murders took place."

The dinner I'd planned went very well. The old guide even volunteered to prepare it for us and we volunteered to let him. We all worked at cleaning the kitchen area sufficiently to allow proper preparation of the meal and a clean area in which to sit and consume it. As he was involved in his meal preparation, Adam and I removed ourselves from the immediate area of the meal preparation—still in the same area but far enough away so whispers would not be overheard. Adam began pretending to discuss sketches of the house he'd made but, quietly, he began to clarify his impression about Karen he'd had earlier in the day. We spoke in very low, cautious voices.

"Karen McNome. The daughter of Brian McNome, master of this house. Karen McNome, the daughter who was slaughtered by a killer within the walls of this house."

I still didn't understand. "That girl I met was no ghost!"

Adam just grinned wider, his eyes sparkled.

I started feeling a little weaker in the stomach. "But the girl I met was real. I mean. I could really touch her and I could feel her touching me." Adam was still grinning. "And besides, Adam, we both know there are no such things as ghosts!"

I was nearly pleading with Adam for an end to his cruel joke. "But, Adam, the girl I met says she loves me!" I hesitated, still not believing Adam. "How could a ghost love me? I don't even believe in ghosts, for crying out loud, how do you expect me to believe that, not only is there such a thing, but one has a crush on me?"

Finally he spoke. "Alex, you and I have been friends for many years and we have investigated many phenomenon and always, always we came to agree there was such a thing as a spiritual essence existing in certain structures which was similar to a snapshot of a traumatic happening at that location. But, in the back of both of our minds was always the belief that ghosts were possible, just not yet experienced. So, although

A House

we never really experienced one before, it was not to say that there was no such thing, right?"

"Right," I mumbled, weakly nodding my head.

He sighed. "I guess now, actively experiencing one, we must change our minds to accept the possibility that ghosts do exist."

I looked up at him. "But how did you know I met Karen?"

He smiled. "I am an empath. A psychic empath. Not only do I sense the paranormal, I experience the feelings of the paranormal. And I could tell she had been with you. I could even see her face!"

He broke into a broad grin. "Alex, this place is so unique! The energy in this house is so strong it excites and terrifies me at the same time!"

Still whispering, I continued, "But Karen…"

"I knew she was here because some of her spiritual impressions were left on you. And I could even smell her perfume on your face!"

I insisted. "But Adam, how could you know that what I experienced was Karen, the ghost, and not Karen, the girl from town?"

His face puzzled a bit. "I'm not sure. I guess it's because I sensed the energy left with you was an ethereal energy." His face still had a curious look on it. "And the spiritual imprint was not of this earth."

We turned our attention to the guide who was still busy preparing a meal for us and bragging about how good it was going to be. How difficult was it to heat beans from a can and reheat some previously prepared stew and throw out a few dinner rolls? But to humor the guy, we raved about it. Thank goodness for totally disposable everything, including utensils.

While we were eating I had time to rethink the events of the day. Thanks to Adam we knew how two of the family met their deaths. We knew the names of the family members. We knew the name of their killer. We knew the motive for the killings. We knew there were probably two diaries that contained incriminating evidence against the accused. I knew, although Adam did not, that one of the diaries lay in ashes in the fireplace in the library. In all the confusion I had failed to check the fireplace. Adam and I also knew the spiritual energies present in the house were the strongest we had ever experienced in any location. We also knew if the events became any more realistic Adam would be seriously injured. And, for the first time for either of us, we had come to believe in the possibility of true spiritual manifestations: ghosts.

By the time we finished our dinner it was after six. We all shuffled slowly back to the library and I went directly to the fireplace and picked up the ashes of the diary, exactly as Karen had described. Without even thinking, I said, "Well there's not much of this diary left to read."

The guide's hands sprang to clutch his heart and a look of terrible pain covered his face as he staggered back two steps. I rushed to his side and supported him as I helped him to a chair and insisted he sit down. By the time Adam was there the man was already sitting, wheezing long, dry breaths.

"What on earth is wrong? Are you having a heart attack? Do you have a heart condition?"

His face relaxed and his breathing slowed more toward normal. "No. No, I don't have a heart condition. I can't exactly explain what happened. I guess it was the shock of you saying that statement about some kind of diary scared me so much it startled me and my breathing tightened."

He looked at the charred ashes in my hands, still unbelieving, and then up at my eyes. "What makes you think this is a diary? Whose diary would it be if it were a diary?"

I almost blew it. I stopped and looked at Adam for a moment. I put an incredibly stupid look on my face, shrugged my shoulders, and answered, "Lucky guess!" I paused for a moment and looked at Adam and we both started to laugh. I then regained control of myself and tried to think up something better. "I deducted it must be the diary of Brian McNome. Adam had mentioned the man's diary had been a matter of concern when the man was murdered and, of course, due to the shape of the ashes I naturally just assumed it must be that of a diary and, logically, it must be the diary of Brian McNome." I think the phrase to describe my explanation was what we used to call "backpedaling" when we were kids—making something up to match the situation rather than clutter the issue with facts alone.

Adam had created an excuse to allow us to separate again for further investigation. He also understood the importance now of keeping my investigation away from that of the old man. He had suggested, "Alex, why don't you pick up the pace on the investigation again. When our friend here recovers fully from his attack he and I will stick together and continue our investigation as well, all right?"

He had been staring into my eyes in such a way as to say, "This will keep things going in the proper direction and maybe you'll begin pulling clues together." I nodded my head in agreement and started off away from the other two.

Chapter 4
The Basement

I checked once again to be sure that my flashlight was still operable and that I had one spare set of batteries in my pocket, just in case I had to go to spaces where lighting was nonexistent. I still wasn't sure what I was looking for but I knew part of it would be found in the basement and part of it would be found "somewhere else"—where, I had no idea. It's always difficult discovering something when you don't know what it is you're searching for. The old expression that went some thing like, "I don't know where we're going but we're making good time," somehow kept running through my mind. Also constantly running through my mind were thoughts of Karen. Emotionally, I was torn nearly in two. My feelings for her were growing by the second, my fascination with her was growing by leaps and bounds, and my combination of fear and fascination with the whole concept of being loved by a dead girl crammed my head with so much internal noise and strife I nearly fell down a set of dark stairs leading to the basement when I happened to open a door to see where it led.

I kept telling myself that Karen had told me there was a tunnel that was going to be important to solving the mystery and tunnels don't grow above ground very often. So, I convinced myself, I'd have to chance being in the dark and rummaging my way around an even mustier, danker place than the rest of the house. Let me tell you, the other parts of the house were Holiday Inn compared to the basement with its rats, bugs, water, mildew, mold, occasional snake, and a smell you'd have to experience to understand. It was as close as I could imagine to what it would be like to be buried for a couple years, wake up inside your coffin, and experience all those nice sensations like wet earth, worms, water, rot, the whole pepperoni. Sure, I felt just fine. The place was so dark my flashlight beam appeared to be a solid, powdery white rod stretching in front of me. The humidity was so high the beam did not diverge much and so not much light spread around the room as I walked. And every step I took made an exploding cloud of thick dust rise from the floor.

The floor was a combination of flagstones and earth randomly covered with items that either fell from the floor/ceiling above or from tables, walls, or shelves in the close vicinity to where I walked. And, like the casket experience I mentioned earlier, it was deathly quiet as well. There was no sound from above, below, around, other than the pounding of my heart in my ears and the occasional sigh I'd make to bolster my fading courage.

Different from most basements I'd been in before, this one was broken into many small rooms, very few having doors but all having doorways. As much as I could, I looked over every inch of the spaces I passed through. Every shelf was examined for signs of anything like a personal effect. Every drawer was opened, no matter how slimy and difficult. No diaries. No personal papers. Plenty of pill bugs, spiders, and snakes. And then there was the constant reminder I

A House

really wasn't alone—the scratchy sound of mice and rats scurrying around did little to bolster my courage.

There was a room full of old toys. I'd guessed those must have been Karen's when she was a child. I looked around and saw items that all seemed to support a central theme pertaining to dolls and horses. In one corner of the room was a wall covered with shelves, every shelf was jammed with model horses. Another corner had a table with a dollhouse, dolls of the proper scale thoughtfully placed in appropriate positions. But the largest play area was a table that took nearly half the room. It was covered in what appeared to be dolls. I moved to the table and looked at the collection of dolls all having porcelain faces and once neat, well maintained dresses. I picked up the prettiest one and, wiped the years of dirt from its face. Looking into its eyes I said aloud, "Karen, I can just picture you playing with this little lady when you were a tot."

Very softly, far behind me, probably near where the doorway was to the room, a woman's voice just above a whisper answered me. "That was my favorite doll. Her name is Tessy."

A warm front of shock rolled over me but, this time, not fear. I turned around and saw Karen standing in the darkness. My first instinct was to put the beam of the flashlight on her but, remembering what she had said earlier, I left it resting on the table supporting itself, its beam pointing at the ceiling and giving a soft glow to the room.

This time I could see Karen quite well. She was even more beautiful than I'd imagined and much better than her photograph had made her look. And the look in her eyes told me she cared deeply about me and was

G. Voyten

touched with my softness toward the doll and my thoughts of her. I slowly, cautiously, walked over to her. My hand reached out and softly touched her face and, much to my surprise, her hand did the same to me. Our eyes were glued on each other's in a type of mutual fascination.

I couldn't help it. I spoke. "Karen, you're undoubtedly the most beautiful lady I have ever seen. And I ... love you, too."

She smiled and a sparkle gleamed in her eyes. "I've waited a long time to hear someone say that. I am so glad the someone was you, the man I love."

I took both her hands in mine and questioned, "But how can you be a ghost? How can I touch you and talk to you as though you are alive?"

She gently smiled again. "Because, to you, I ***am*** alive! Your mind makes me live!" She chuckled to herself. "Spirits are around the living all the time! The living do not see because they do not believe in themselves, let alone those who are not whole."

I know my face probably looked troubled because that was how my mind felt. But I had to pursue it. "But, Karen, before Adam and I discussed you I didn't even believe in the existence of ghosts! Why, then, could I experience you?"

Her face softened even more. "Maybe because our spirits have mingled for many years, waiting for the call to allow us to be joined physically."

"Is that why I felt like I knew you even when I saw you for the first time?"

"Yes, it is. Although we have not physically been together before, we have been together spiritually for many years and will remain together for eternity."

A House

I hesitated. "Can I ... hug you?"

She shyly smiled. Quietly, softly, she said, "I would like that."

I took her deep into my arms and she molded her body against mine. We could not have been closer together if we had tried. Even her face molded itself into the side of mine. I just stood there holding her for what seemed like an eternity. I kept holding and squeezing her closer, my hands running through her hair, across her back, and we swayed back and forth a little, so intimate an act my eyes closed, as though kissing, so comfortable in the act it was almost impossible to let it end. And then I felt her hands behind me, rubbing my back, my neck, my hair. I felt the gentlest kiss on my neck as though she wanted to have it without me knowing she had done so.

When we drew away to where I could see her face I immediately kissed her, long, tender, sincere, warm. I took her face in my hands and played with her hair. When I drew away a silvery tear was sliding down her right cheek.

She sobbed. "I'm sorry. It is very difficult when you love someone so much and know you can not remain with them for many years yet to come."

Still holding her face in one hand and stroking her long yellow hair with my other hand I replied, "You don't think I will ever leave this place now, do you? Even if you are not whole, you are still the best thing that has ever happened to me!"

Another tear ran down her cheek. "It cannot be. If you do not solve the curse, I will still be forced to relive my death every night for eternity. You must not think of the small joy we might have for today but the greater joy you could bring us all by releasing us from our curse. My father already accepts you for your courage and remarkable spiritual perception. He accepts Adam because he is the catalyst. He accepts the guide because he is a key element in the curse. But he will not allow me to love a living man if it means continuing the curse on all those forced to roam this house." She hesitated. Her head lowered. "And I cannot expect to stay with you. Even if the curse is not broken, I cannot tell if I will ever be allowed to be with you again."

"Then I must never leave this house alive!" I insisted. "I will not leave you!"

She was crying more now and her bottom lip quivered. "No, no please don't think like that. Maybe Father will change his mind once the curse is released." She sobbed. "And, even if the curse does not end, there might be a way for us to remain together."

I held her close to me, feeling the cold tears soaking into my shoulder. I kissed her wet cheek. "Then let us hold that belief strong in our minds. Let us hope this curse can be lifted and our souls can be eternally together. Or another way can be found to allow us to stay together." I pulled back from her a bit so I could look into her tear-pooled eyes. "Ok?"

She sniffed her nose a little and smiled through the tears. "Yes, we must believe." Her hand stroked the side of my face. "But let me be your companion while you are here. Let us enjoy this night as much as we can in spite of the circumstances." She kissed me lightly but lovingly. "Let us be lovers and best friends for the present in case this night is the first and last night we will have until we meet again under equal conditions."

A House

I held her a little longer. I just didn't want to let go of her for fear she would be gone. I stood there, eyes closed, trying to make a mental picture of everything about her to remember forever. Her smell—that wonderful, sweet, powdery smell—like hugging a baby. Her softness. The touch of her skin was like having my face next to satin. Her hair was as soft as silk and smelled like herbs. And her body was soft and supple. I liked the way it responded to my hugs, the way it conformed to my shape like it was part of me.

I whispered to her. "Are you going to be able to stay with me while I'm down here looking around?" I could feel her head nodding as it lay against mine. "Are you going to be able to stay with me later this night when I am upstairs, away from the others?" Again, her head nodded. I squeezed her closer. "Then we must make the most of this glorious opportunity together."

I dried her tears and she looked up at me and weakly smiled. I could not help but see the combination of love and sadness in her eyes. Something made me feel we would not see each other after the curse was lifted. She felt that way as well and she did not want me to know it. I did not indicate I understood such for fear it would not make parting any easier. However, I felt the lifting of the curse would mean, as one might assume, there would no longer be any reason for her restless spirit to roam the house. She would probably go to wherever spirits go, for, surely, there must be a place. If ever there were a reason to begin believing in an afterlife this experience would have been it. If there were no life after death, there would be no entity to "haunt" the house.

Without further discussion about the inevitable, I changed the subject as I picked up the flashlight and we headed out of the room and back down the dark hallway. "So where are your mom and dad right now?"

She put an arm around my waist as we walked and I did the same to her. "Oh, right now they are keeping an eye on your companions."

I laughed a little. "Do you think they would allow me to meet them?" Ha, I thought. Fat chance.

She turned toward me in the darkness. "Would you really like to meet them?" Even in the darkness I could see she was smiling.

I'd shocked even myself. Oh, brother! What was I getting myself into? But I sheepishly asked, "Do you think they would?"

She beamed! "Yes! Yes, they would love to meet you!"

She disappeared so quickly it was as though she had never been there. It startled me so severely I began to doubt my own sanity at even thinking she had been present! But, as quickly as she had disappeared, she reappeared ahead of me out of the beam of the flashlight, two others with her, one to each side.

"Alex, Mother and Father are here but request you not place your light on them for they fear it."

I put the flashlight on the dirt floor pointing toward the wall parallel to my direction of travel. Again, it gave a soft glow to the hallway but not harsh, direct lighting. The three dark shapes from the far end of the hall approached. I was petrified! As the shapes got closer I became more uncomfortable. It was not just the thought of seeing two additional apparitions, it was

A House

more like the feeling of meeting your girl's parents for the first time and I was afraid the reception was not going to be very good. Sure, in the real world parents could say you weren't good enough for their daughter because you were poor, black, Irish, Hispanic, something. I was afraid this condemnation would be more like, "We were really hoping she would bring home someone more like her present state of existence." And how could I argue that point?

Brian McNome was a stern man. His face constantly scowled, not because of me but because of the state of his existence. He was angry. <u>Very</u> angry. His whole spiritual existence was intent on revenge against the man who destroyed his beautiful family. But, I thought, I would try to convince the man I was there to help him, not just interfere or brag about being in the home. However, his conversation with me was nothing like I'd expected!

Brian was dressed, strangely, in a jacket, like a "smoking jacket," complete with satin collar and rich colors. He was not an unusually tall man but his features were strong and attractive. My feeling about him was his looks were appealing to other men as a "man's man" look. His eyes, as well as I could tell, were gray and clear and his dark hair contrasted with his fair skin. And, lucky for me, if ghosts were supposed to continue looking like they did at the time of death, then he had looked fine. More likely, I thought, they might appear as they had just before their death.

Sarah McNome was a beautiful woman, soft, well mannered, pure class. I could tell Karen got her looks from her mother for the two of them together looked more like beautiful sisters than mother and daughter. Her mother's face, however, was perpetually saddened. I wasn't sure if it was because of their present spiritual state or if, like mothers everywhere, she knew of Karen's feelings toward me and the futility of the relationship. Her hair and complexion matched that of Karen's and even her shape was similar. At whatever age she represented she still was the image of a beautiful woman.

Sarah McNome's dress was understated elegance. I couldn't make out what the fabric was but it was attractive and the cut and lay of it spoke of custom tailoring. Sarah's features, like Karen's, were stunning. She appeared to be middle aged but of such striking beauty she could have passed for a woman of many fewer years.

To me, it was obvious the family had class, much more than any of the villagers I had met. They all carried themselves with the posture of self confidence that must be mastered in life from successes, not failures. Their air of control told me all had had lives where they were used to being obeyed without question. I am not trying to say they were aloof or arrogant but proud and strong willed.

I decided to begin the conversation. "It is a great honor to meet you both, Mr. and Mrs. McNome."

Mr. McNome began immediately in what was to be a very interesting conversation. "We are pleased to make your acquaintance as well, son. I was very pleased when Karen told me you requested meeting the Mrs. and myself." He smiled a little. "You are the first mortal who has wanted to see us since we passed on to this spirit world. The rest of the mortal world has

A House

preferred to think us too terrifying to understand." He smiled again. "But you must understand, son, you are a special, chosen man. Others, including your gifted friend, Adam, cannot see or experience us the way you can. Although Adam can relive events when he comes in contact with the point of the psychic energy deposit he would never be able to experience us as you can. It is your ability that allows us to appear whole, solid, alive, not his. So, you see, it is <u>you</u> that is the most gifted, not your friend, Adam!"

I felt my legs weakening and I was trying with all my might to keep from passing out. I had never been so terrified in my life. No, it was not just the fact that I was apparently talking to ghosts of three who died sixty years before; it was the nature of the revelations and the conditions of the conversation. I though I should continue with just a few more courtesies before getting down to the real work at hand. "Please let me say how sorry I am that the three of you had such tragic deaths and that your souls were forced to roam this earth these last sixty years. Please believe me when I say I will do everything in my power to break this curse and allow you revenge on your killer."

All three smiled. Mr. McNome put his arm around his wife and Karen came over to my side and put her arm around me as well. I was shocked Karen would do that in front of her father! I whispered to her immediately. "Karen! Your father's wishes..."

She smiled shyly. "He knows, Alex. He's always known. But I couldn't tell you. You see, you could only see him if you were the one requesting it!"

I was even more confused. "But he knows how we feel about each other?" I whispered.

She giggled. She whispered back, "Yes. He has known for the last sixty years how much I've loved you."

I was even more confused. "Karen! I'm not even thirty years old! How could you feel that way about me longer than I've been alive?"

Mr. McNome interjected. "Because spirits are always alive. She met you spiritually long before your mother bore you."

I know I must have had a rather blank look on my face. "I'm trying to understand," I answered.

"And that brings me to another point I must tell you. When you leave this place in the morning—and you will leave this place in good health in the morning—you must take the evidence you gather to a lawyer in the village. The law office of Smith and Edwards has controlled the estate since my death. You must present all the evidence to that office and stay there until told to depart. Is that understood?"

I nodded my head. "Yes, sir. I understand."

He continued. "That is why this property was not turned over to the state. The property, in the event of our deaths, was turned over to the legal firm until the surviving members of a branch of my family could be located to transfer ownership over to them."

"But was there any member of that family left? Why would it take them sixty years to find someone?"

"It might be due to the fact the addresses of the family were not recorded anywhere in our community and the lawyers had to contact many different agencies to locate these people. Or there is the possibility the family name was, somehow, changed but I cannot assure you of the reason. It is difficult to explain the

A House

events of the living when you are prisoner to an ethereal plane."

I nodded again. "I understand, sir. I'm sorry for such ignorance ..."

He smiled. "It is understandable. How many times do the living have conversations with the dead or even attempt to understand the concept? But now I must tell you some of the things you might need to solve this curse and release our souls from this house. You already know the details about my death and that of my wife and the person responsible for these acts. What you do not yet know is what evidence you must uncover to solve this crime and present to the attorneys."

I held Karen's hand and gave it a squeeze. "Please continue."

"The thief stole money, jewelry, and other negotiables from this house. I heard the old man who has accompanied you to this house mention that no valuables from this house have shown up since stolen from here. That is because the thief, a young man of twenty-two years at the time, returned to the house through the tunnel and hid the items within. The entire value of the stolen items was only about ten thousand dollars at the time of our deaths. I cannot tell you if it would be worth that today or, for that matter, if it would be worth anything. There were at least a million of my dollars in the bank when I died. That money, sitting in bank accounts, has sustained the estate these years since my death and paid the yearly fee to the lawyers for their continuing support of my estate and the search for our relatives. And there are the assets from my business. I cannot say if the business still thrives or has gone broke in my absence. However, within a secret hiding place on these grounds, a million dollars in stocks, bonds, cash money, gold, jewelry, artifacts and paintings, lies to be discovered. The relative will inherit it all, the house, the grounds, the money, the gold, all of it."

My face blanched. Under my breath I muttered, "That'll be one lucky relative!"

Brian answered me as though I'd shouted it at him. Staring deep into my eyes he continued dead seriously (pardon the pun), "You already intimately know the only surviving relative of this family. I feel confident you will not want for reward from this person after the crime is solved and the curse is lifted. Even if money has devalued at a phenomenal rate, I am sure you will not be disappointed in the generosity of this member of my family toward you."

I could feel my face flush with embarrassment as I replied, "Thank you, sir, but I'm very sorry to sound like I'm a greedy, unfeeling person. My original intent for coming here was to investigate the possibility of ghosts in this house at the request of a group of town leaders and to try discovering what was causing the frightening experiences townspeople were having on these premises. My services were free, of course. I guess I have already solved the main reason for being here. However, after Adam discovered the details of the crimes committed here I felt a much deeper, much more important reason for being here: I felt I could not leave here without solving this terrible crime once and for all."

I cleared my throat and continued. "Besides, sir, I am already a successful, relatively wealthy man myself. Although I would take great delight in discovering the secrets of this house and seeing your hidden treasures, I expect nothing for myself other than the satisfaction of knowing I have solved this mystery and, for myself, have confirmed my lifelong question regarding the existence of ghosts."

I felt something was behind me. The hairs on the back of my neck bristled and a chill ran up my spine. I hesitated to ask but felt forced. "Is there ... some other force or spirit here besides the three of you?"

Mrs. McNome answered. "Yes. There are others trapped within the confines of this house as well. This house existed long before we lived here originally. It has been here since before the Civil War. A cemetery exists on the grounds and some of the deceased from that time still roam these halls as well." Her face frowned. "That is why even we cannot absolutely guarantee the safety of you and, especially, your companions. These other spirits are angry with all the living and would enjoy destroying as many of them as they could."

Karen squeezed my hand and grabbed my arm with her other hand and squeezed it as well. "That is why Father thinks it is wise for me to spend as much time with you as possible. As long as I am with you the others know you are a friend of those souls not yet at rest and will not attack you." She stroked my arm lightly and looked down at the dark earthen floor. "I am afraid I cannot make the same statement about your companions. As darkness falls these other restless spirits begin roaming." She again paused and sadly looked up into my eyes. "These spirits will try taking out their vengeance upon you all. They blame the

G. Voyten

living for not only their fates but ours as well. They think they are doing what is right for us and are too embittered to listen to reason."

I sighed and wiped my brow with my free hand. "Please continue, Mr. McNome. Please tell me what you feel you must in order to set things right." I paused for a moment and, before Mr. McNome had a chance to begin I had thought of one last frightening question: "If we solve your crime and release your curse, what will become of the spirits of the others? Will they continue to haunt the living or will they, too, abandon this earth and go to their ultimate resting place?"

Mrs. McNome answered immediately. "We have never thought about that." She looked at her husband for a moment and, without further hesitation, continued, "While you are discussing things with my good husband I will go and speak with these others and see if I might find a solution to their dilemma." And with that she slowly disappeared back into the utter blackness of the end of the hallway.

Mr. McNome picked up the conversation again. "In order to break the curse you must collect a series of clues to turn over to the lawyers. First, you must recover the stolen valuables hidden somewhere in this house. Second, you must find the hidden diary belonging to my daughter. You must insure it still contains the evidence of the guilt of Elias Johnson. We had suspected for weeks before the murders that the man had been pilfering from the house. Third, you must find the three murder weapons used in the crimes. Please remember to handle them in such a way so as not to obscure the clues each may hold. Fourth, you must show evidence of my daughter's death to lay to

A House

rest the claims she actually murdered us and stole the money and ran away. The rest of the village doubts she died since no evidence was ever found in the house during the preliminary police investigation documenting the fact that Karen did, in fact, die within the confines of this structure. And, finally, you must find the whereabouts of this Elias Johnson and bring back evidence to this house and to the lawyers of his demise or, if he still lives, bring him back into the confines of this house to face his crimes."

I shook my head. "Mr. McNome, you ask a lot, you know."

He nodded sadly. "I know, son. I understand how you must feel. But I will allow you the liberty of keeping my loving daughter with you as a constant companion to assist you in your quest for these items. None of us are able to identify where all these items are located but Karen will aid you in any way she is capable. And, when the time comes, she will guide you to the spot of her death, as you witnessed such with my good wife and myself."

I lowered my head. I doubted they had the right man for the job. "I understand, sir." I looked up at him, as determined as I could be. "I will do my very best."

His majestic shape began to fade as though walking back into the distant darkness at the end of the hallway, although his legs were not moving. His voice, fading away as did his image, whispered, "I know you will do your best, son. I have the greatest confidence in you…"

I watched the spot where he was until there was nothing left to see. When his image was completely gone I briefly looked at the floor where he and his wife had been standing and noticed they had not made a mark in the thick dust of the floor, as I had with my own steps. I turned to look at Karen. She stood there staring at me and I'd come to feel she had been doing so the entire time I'd been talking to her father.

I smiled weakly at her. "What are you staring at?"

A tear again pooled in her eye and rolled down her cheek. "I am trying to learn your face to remember you as strongly as I can in case I never see you again after this night." She turned and hugged me tightly, laying her face again on my shoulder and sobbing deeply. "I will miss you so much I can barely conceive of ever leaving you."

I stroked her hair with one hand and held her close with the other. "Let's not waste our time thinking of when we will not be together again but cherish these few hours we will share with each other."

I pulled away a little to look into her face but she would not let her eyes look at me. Instead, she looked down, defeated. She nodded slightly and sobbed deeply again. I put one hand beneath her chin and lifted her head until she was looking into my eyes. When she finally looked at me I tenderly kissed her and squeezed her close to me.

"Besides," I added, "who is to say you will leave me forever? You said yourself that the spirit never dies, never leaves, didn't you?"

She nodded, a small smile forming on her lips.

I smiled back. "Then what is to say that, even after your spirit is freed from the curse, you cannot still be free to visit me?"

A House

She jumped toward me and wrapped her arms around me tightly. "Oh, Alex, I knew you'd find a way to make me feel better!"

I picked up the flashlight from the floor and we started down the hallway. No, she assured me, there was no reason she could think of to check each of the rooms in the basement for clues. She was anxious to show me the tunnel. However, I corrected her. There was also the other evidence we had to be concerned with. We needed to discover the items used in the murders of her family. She agreed and we began systematically checking the rooms.

A room filled with home canned goods. Karen's mother insisted her canned vegetables were the best because of the care she took in their preparation. Karen boasted, "My mother made the best tomato sauce with hot peppers of anyone in town."

I looked at the cans. "I'd say these jars are a little too old to try." I picked up one container and the top had completely rotted out and crumbled to the floor. Luckily, I didn't get any of the contents on me as it gurgled out of the jar.

Another room was full of clothing. The room, not opened in sixty years, still smelled strongly of the cedar walls of which it was built. The clothing within this relatively airtight room was still in very good shape. There were no dust or dirt or spider webs. It was like finding an airtight tomb from long ago that time had not been able to touch. It was quite an unusual feeling!

The door behind us abruptly slammed shut! I was nearly terrified out of my skin at the intensity of the impact the door made with the jam. As I turned toward the opening I noticed there was no apparent door handle—no visible way out!

I looked at Karen. She had a look mixed between anger and fear. "That was no accident! One of our old Civil War friends decided you would become a permanent resident of this air tight room!" She reached over to where the door handle would have been if there had been a door handle and turned an "invisible" knob. The door quietly swung open and we left. I sighed and smiled at Karen, thinking how fortunate it had been having her there!

One large open area had a furnace system for the house. In the dark distance there was a coal bin. I asked Karen if she would mind us looking a little closer at the coal bin. Why, she wanted to know. I explained the possibility Elias Johnson might have chosen the coal to dig into to hide the weapons or the money.

I looked around the coal bin. After just a little investigation I could see what I could only call a bump in the otherwise evenly angled slanting pile of coal. I moved a few pieces of the coal and, in about five minutes, discovered clothing. Clothing? I surmised it might be the clothing worn during one of the murders where blood might have been splattered on the murderer. "We'll take this with us, at any rate," I told Karen.

I dug around in the coal for a longer time to see if the murder weapons or the stolen money might also be there. But, after an additional ten minutes of digging, I had no such luck.

Five more rooms. Five more examples of wasted time. Finally, Karen pointed at a door in a strange

A House

room filled with doors. It appeared to be a room for entertaining. "Behind that door should be the tunnel that leads off the property."

Chapter 5
The Tunnel

I put the flashlight down so it pointed toward the wall and began moving items from in front of the wooden door. It appeared someone wanted this particular door to appear unusable by stacking things in front of it. And, in about fifteen minutes, the opening was cleared and we opened the door leading to the tunnel and prepared to continue into the tunnel. The clothing I had accumulated from the coal pile was left on a chair in that room. We could recover it later but I really didn't want any chance of things carried interfering with my ability to react quickly later if necessary.

Karen balked. I asked what was the problem. She replied there was someone in the tunnel that she did not like. Was he alive or dead, I asked. He was dead, she said. Did she know who he was and what his problem was, I asked.

"He was a vagabond from the village who wandered into the tunnel for shelter and died of cold one winter many years ago. Mother and I have always been afraid of him because he is bitter toward us for not taking him in to feed him when he was alive."

"Did he ask for shelter from you?" I asked.

"Well, not directly," she replied. "Actually he'd asked one of the staff."

"Which one?" I wondered.

A House

She thought about it for a moment and then turned to me in horror. "Elias Johnson!"

I started down the tunnel pulling Karen in with me. She still was terrified to continue but I assured her I'd handle it when the time came. "Will I be able to see him?" I asked.

She looked at me. "Do you want to see him?"

I couldn't believe I was answering, "Sure I want to see him!"

She looked at me in disbelief. And then, with doubt in her voice, she replied, "Then you will see him!"

The tunnel was rounded at the top and the floor, although pretty flat, was also rounded. I was more uncomfortable with all the rats and snakes zipping around by my feet than the possibility of seeing another ghost. Strange. Although before that day I had never seen a ghost, there I was, only a few hours later, unfettered about seeing one that was supposed to be a nasty one!

We had probably gone about three hundred feet before a voice pierced the darkness ahead of us. "Where do you think you're going?"

I could just barely make out the black shape of a hulking man waddling toward us out of the darkness. The closer he came, the more light from behind him there appeared to be. His shadow started stretching long before him giving him the appearance of being much larger than he actually was. His eyes seemed to glow red like a light was shined into his retinas and the red reflected back. His image was black, even blacker than the tunnel darkness itself and it didn't appear there was a true body to go with that darkness for a long, terrifying while. The walls seemed to be hissing like ocean foam. "We're looking for a man we're going to punish," I yelled back. "He's the handyman here. Maybe you know him. His name is Elias Johnson. We're going to punish him for mistreating people in need that came to our door for help that he turned away without telling the family."

All of a sudden the hulking man stopped dead in his tracks and stood straighter. He looked like he was trying to run his fingers through his hair to comb it and then he tried to hit the dust out of his clothing as we continued to approach. The hissing subsided.

I kept the flashlight pointed down at the ground, as the McNomes had taught me earlier. We got right up next to the man and I placed my hand firmly on his shoulder with a pat that raised a cloud of dust. The touch was startlingly cold to my hand, like grabbing ice itself. My voice was low and compassionate. "I think you will find that the lady of the house, Mrs. Sarah McNome, is waiting upstairs in the kitchen with a plate of food for you right now, my friend. Please let her help you and any of your friends in need."

The evil, filthy, vengeful look on his face disappeared and a look of surprise and delight replaced it. "Really?" he asked. His voice had changed from one threatening violence to one of benevolence.

Karen sighed a big sigh and nodded her head as she smiled. "Really!" she piped.

The man took my hand and shook it until I thought it would come off. The temperature of his grip changed from icy to only moderately cold, like room temperature. "Thank you! Thank you, my good sir! I cannot thank you enough! You have saved my life! You have rekindled my faith in humanity!"

A House

I shook hands with him firmly and with great feeling. I again patted his shoulder. Looking him straight in the eye I gently added, "Never give up on mankind, my good fellow, for the shortcomings of one are not the shortcomings of all."

Tears poured from his withered face and down his bristled, unshaven cheeks. "God bless you, sir! And God bless this generous household and all who live within it!"

I left him saying, "And God bless and keep you as well, my friend. And may you find peace on this earth and the next."

The man hobbled away from us going toward the house, his ghostly image changing from the darkest black toward white, as though his very soul had change from the dark side of humanity toward the light. His voice was echoing through the tunnel as he disappeared in the darkness as he continued to say over and over, "God bless this house and all who live within. God bless this house and all who live within…"

Karen and I watched as he literally dematerialized as he walked away. In a very dry, whisper she said, "He is no more a spirit trapped in this house. His curse has been lifted. He has gone to his final rest." She looked up at me, a tear in her eye. "You have freed his misguided soul from the damnation of this house!"

I exhaled a long, relaxing breath. "It's my feeling right now that all the restless spirits trapped within the confines of this house and property only need a reason to believe their conflict is no longer valid. I'm hoping that, one by one, I can resolve the conflicts and release their souls."

She looked at me doubtingly. "But you could not possibly do all that within the confines of a single evening! There are probably a dozen souls trapped in this house! How could you possibly meet every condition of their curses within one single evening?"

We started walking again and I didn't even look at her. "I would have to spend additional nights in the house and hope the spirits would not kill me before letting me understand their problems and help them toward solutions."

She squeezed my hand and continued to hold it. "The more I know you, the better I like you. I am so pleased to understand you would put the conflicts of others so high on your list of life priorities with nothing to gain for yourself other than a clear conscience."

We hadn't walked many more feet down the tunnel before we found the physical remains of the soul we had encountered just minutes earlier. A body, still laying in a fetal position on the ground, probably attempting to stay warm, still there after sixty years of silent misery.

We slowly continued walking down the tunnel. The darkness and humidity alone felt unnerving and overbearing but, even beyond that, I still had an incredibly tight feeling of fear in my chest about events approaching us in the tunnel just ahead.

Karen felt the tension in the hand of mine she held and she asked about it. "Your muscles are rigid in your hand and arm. You fear something ahead, don't you?"

I sighed. "Karen, I feel something ahead but I can't explain it to you. I feel … <u>evil</u>. The farther we go, the more evil I feel awaiting. It's like seeing death itself

A House

staring you in the face and it frightens me. I don't know how to deal with it."

She squeezed my hand tighter and her other hand squeezed the upper part of my arm. She pulled herself closer and was practically leaning against me as we walked, very slowly. "I can feel it, too. It frightens me as well because, like you, I feel it is a force of great evil that even I cannot overcome."

"Do you think it is a spirit?" I whispered.

"No, no I think it is more like that psychic energy your companion, Adam, detects. It is like the gates of Hell themselves. It is a very powerful negative emotional force concentrated in a place, not a person or spirit. I feel like being in this place or touching anything around it would hurt me or affect me. It frightens me!"

Maybe it was my imagination, maybe not, but the farther we went the shorter the beam of my flashlight pierced the darkness until, as we approached what appeared to be a small side tunnel to the main tunnel, the beam of the flashlight only illuminated a couple feet directly in front of us and nothing to either side of the main beam. The closer we got to the side tunnel, the harder it was for me to breathe. Even Karen appeared to have a difficult time breathing and I knew that was impossible! A low moaning started and grew as we approached and the very humidity of the tunnel grew overpowering. The walls began hissing, as before.

Karen commented on the little side tunnel, actually turning out to be more of a room than just a tunnel. "This little room was used as a storage area for yard and garden implements. Other than the family members, only the handyman knew of this place and this tunnel. He also mowed the lawns and took care of the grounds and machines."

Through the all-encompassing blackness of the small room we could barely make out the contents of what was within. The moaning grew louder and the air grew thicker making moving around more difficult. Yes, there were lawn equipment and garden implements and various containers and tools. But, eventually, as we made our way around the room, the feeling of destruction—of death itself—became so overpowering we could hardly breathe. And, by the time we were in a corner of the room the farthest from the opening to the tunnel, not only was the feeling of impending doom nearly overpowering but the beam of the flashlight—my only physical proof that what was happening was not just in my mind—illuminated only the area directly in front of its lens no more than six inches away. I felt it might only have been the batteries weakening but that moment was not a grand time to test my theory.

And then I spotted it. Low, in the corner, behind a stack of shovels and rakes, I saw a toolbox and clothing lying atop it. Before I had a chance to say a word, Karen blurted out, "The handyman's toolbox!"

I began moving away the tools that were covering the toolbox. My breathing was labored to the point I thought the room must be void of air and the laboring was due to my becoming asphyxiated. My arms and hands moved in slow motion like a force stronger than mine was resisting them. But, eventually, the corner was cleared and the toolbox and other items came into view.

A House

As poorly as I had been feeling, I felt worse as soon as I touched the first item in the corner for the very density of the room seemed to change and the low pitched moan of doom was now practically yelling out of the very walls and continued to grow in volume as I moved the items from the corner out into the room. The floor seemed to soften and stick to my feet like hot tar.

Karen was holding my arm so tightly I was losing circulation in it. She began tugging at me. "This is very bad," she yelled, just above the moaning. She pulled at my arm much more frantically. Louder and more urgently, she yelled to be heard above the intense moaning, "Let's get out of here now! We cannot exist in here much longer! Grab the evidence and leave with me now!"

The moaning grew to a loud roar as though many voices were joining in the fray. The thick air became active and a wind from nowhere began screaming around us, objects becoming airborne in the intensity. As I grabbed the items from the corner and we turned to leave, objects from the walls fell to the floor and the very floor began to move, the items themselves felt like they were burning or biting into my fingers!

We launched ourselves toward the doorway visible dimly in the distance as small hand tools and cutters began throwing themselves at us and bounced off walls around us. The moaning grew even louder and the very smell of the room changed. The floor now felt like it was covered with something trying to hold us back, like hands grabbing at our legs as we tried to run away. The shouting of the room seemed to be saying, "NO!" and "GET OUT" at the same time!

When we got to the tunnel we turned toward the end leading outside, away from the house, rather than back toward it. We continued running down the tunnel, sliding on the slippery, moldy floor, for another hundred feet as we could hear groans and shuddering continuing in the room we had left, echoing from the walls of the tunnel, and items still smashing into the walls of the room and out into the tunnel itself. But the farther away we ran, the more silent the room became.

As we slowed to a walk I noticed the light from the flashlight had miraculously returned to a rather full beam again. Obviously, it was not the batteries causing the dimming experienced within the storage room.

We got to the end of the tunnel. There, a wrought iron gate covered the entrance and was rusted shut. Karen stopped walking with me as we approached the light of day beyond. She was never allowed to enter the light of day, she told me, and that was why she and the other spirits did not like the beam of the flashlight.

I asked her if she would wait while I examined the items we'd collected from the tunnel storage room. She agreed. We knelt, still well within the deep shadows of the tunnel, away from the warmth of the evening setting sun, and quickly examined the contents of the toolbox and bundle of clothing we'd retrieved.

I carefully opened the toolbox first, making sure I didn't obscure fingerprints that might be left behind from the murderer. There, immediately in front of us, was a major part of the puzzle: many hundreds of dollars in cash and stocks and bonds were crammed in where tools should have been. I removed the top carry shelf and the entire bottom of the toolbox was crammed with more of the same. However, at the very

A House

bottom of it all were Sarah's jewelry and the large hunting knife that Karen claimed was the one that had killed Sarah McNome, the stains of her blood still covering the blade.

I hadn't even reached for the knife, only attempted to pull back the money, when Karen, out of concern, blurted out, "Don't touch the knife! You may destroy its evidence!"

I laughed, "Don't worry about me! I wasn't going to touch it!"

We looked at the bundle of clothing that had been setting atop the toolbox. It was difficult to tell what the clothing had originally looked like because of the massive bloodstains covering all of the items.

A voice came from deeper within the tunnel, echoing eerily off the tunnel walls that frightened me to bits. I turned and it was Mr. and Mrs. McNome standing behind us, walking slowly toward us. "Those are the clothes worn by our murderer when my wife and I were butchered in that room where you discovered them," he said. "The knife in the toolbox was just one implement used to sever our bodies apart in that very room. Other implements exist but they can be uncovered later."

He looked down at me with a stern but fond look. "You did well, son. A very important part of the curse has been handled."

He looked into the toolbox. "But this is not all the money that was stolen. This is but a small part. This is only the money that was stolen the day my good wife was murdered. The murderer must have hidden the remainder somewhere else."

I assured him we would continue to search for more of the valuables missing. He only answered that he knew I would do all that was necessary to break the curse.

The sun had settled beneath the horizon and the sky outside was quickly darkening. The wind was picking up and I would have guessed a storm was approaching but for knowing no storms were due to strike the community that day.

Before Mr. and Mrs. McNome disappeared back into the eternal darkness of the tunnel I asked Mr. McNome if he thought there was more reason to return to the storage room and search for more. "No, son, do not risk your very soul by returning to that room at this time. That room is evil itself and it has had sixty years of untamed violence building within its walls. You have already imperiled the souls of yourself and my daughter just by challenging the evil in that place once. Do not chance losing your eternal soul to evil itself by a second challenge."

"But Mr. McNome, how can the evil of that room ever be removed?"

He laughed a laugh I would call "evil" if not for the fact I didn't feel Mr. McNome was an evil man. "When the curse of this house is broken, when Elias Johnson's soul has been laid to unrest, the curse upon him will just begin." He looked up toward the crumbling, falling ceiling of the tunnel and laughed so loudly it echoed the entire length of the tunnel. Smiling, he continued, "When Elias Johnson's soul is turned over to this house, all the evil damnation created within these walls will rest on his eternally cursed soul! You see, he will carry all the evil this

A House

house possesses with him for all eternity! If you wish to call that 'Hell' then I guess that would be as close as one could describe it…"

I rose from the floor of the tunnel to head back toward the house with Karen. By the time I was on my feet and had helped her to hers the image of her mother and father had already departed.

I looked at Karen in this brighter, natural lighting before we disappeared back into the total darkness of the tunnel. Her long, thick, light yellow hair laid in feathery wisps around her soft pink face. Her perky blue-green eyes were set deep within her light skin and her fair brows framed them softly. Her eyes told me she must have been one of the gentlest people I had ever met. Her nose was small and fine and was framed by two perfect high cheekbones. Her lips were dark pink and shiny, still embracing a broad smile. Her white teeth glistened in the light and contrasted perfectly with her lips. Her dress, some kind of print with small geometric characters in it, was round cut at the neck low enough to show her two collar bones just above and a gentle pattern of lace along its edge.

Her body, small and delicate, was squeezed into this dress that conformed closely to her body to the waist where it then blossomed into a loose fullness all the way to the floor. It was obvious to me she was very much a lady and everything about her spoke of breeding, class, and gentility.

She stared at me in disbelief. "What are you doing? Why are you looking at me like that?"

"You've had years to look at me from a distance. I've only known you for a little while and always in near total darkness. Am I not allowed to study you in as much interest and detail as you studied me?"

She blushed and looked down and away from me. "I guess!"

"Besides, since I cannot make a photograph of you and I cannot take you with me for the remainder of my days, I want to remember as much about you as I can!"

She sheepishly looked up at me. Quietly, almost under her breath, she answered, "I understand."

We held hands and I gathered up all the items and we started back for the house. When the tunnel got so dark I had to turn the flashlight back on I had to carry it in one hand and all the other items in the other. Karen held onto my arm with both of hers as we slowly made our way back into the house.

When we passed the storage room the evil in the place, again, grew as we approached. The moaning grew and the air tightened and I could feel the very floor moving beneath my feet. I feared I would fall in the goop covering the floor as we briskly walked by. The walls hissed and, the little I could make out from the reduced beam of the flashlight, the walls were running wet with liquid. Water? Blood? I wasn't about to stop and find out!

As we hastily made our way past the room we could feel an icy wind blowing out of it and items slammed the tunnel wall behind us as we stepped by. I very briefly stopped to look back at the tunnel floor. Half a dozen gardening implements were strewn about; a pair of gardening shears was sticking out of the tunnel wall. I looked at Karen in the dark. "I know those things couldn't hurt you much, but it could have

A House

brought us together a lot quicker than we'd planned if I'd stepped by that place just a little slower!"

She saw no humor in my comment. She replied as we briskly continued away, "That's not funny! Alex, you must be careful! Not only do I not want you hurt because I love you but you must remember the fate of this house, the fortune, the souls of those trapped here, and the lives of your friends depends on you staying alive and removing this curse!"

I tried to laugh it off. "Take it easy! I won't let things get out of hand! Do you think I'd let the bad guys win?"

She was still frowning. "It's not like they're playing a game! Alex, they mean business! A wrong move, a slow reaction, one time being in the wrong place at the wrong time, and you and your friends could join us here instantly!" She looked at me sternly. "What do you think would have happened if I had not been with you in the cedar closet? You would still be there and probably would have run out of fresh air within an hour or two!"

And then her face softened. She sighed. "I'm sorry, Alex. I sound like I'm preaching." She looked up at me with a smile weakly on her lips. Softly, she continued, "I only fear so much for your life because I care so much."

I smiled at her. Softly I replied, "I know, I know. I'm just making light of this because it scares me to pieces. But, inside, I'm still pretty scared! I guess I shouldn't sound like I'm not concerned because, believe me, I'm concerned!"

When we got back into the basement Karen felt it would be best to restack the items in front of the door leading to the tunnel. Why? "I fear for anyone accidentally discovering this entrance and foolish enough to travel into the storage room of evil."

I thought about it. She was probably right. A room like that one could kill an empath like Adam and, I felt, even others, like myself, would eventually fall prey to its power. I felt that, had I spent much more time inside that room, I would probably have passed out and then perished at the hands of the evil unopposed by my will to resist.

We eventually headed for the stairs going up but Karen hesitated. I turned to her with a questioning look on my face. She answered my unspoken question. "I cannot go upstairs with you right now. I don't want to be around the others."

"But I don't want you to leave me!" I complained.

She "tisked" me, very slowly shook her head from side to side, and grinned ear to ear. "I won't be far away! I promise! And neither will the other members of my family! We all care about you!" She paused and her face sobered. "You're still our only hope."

Before I headed up the stairs she stopped me, held me, and kissed me warmly and a little passionately. I could tell her courage with me was building. When we finally separated from the kiss and embrace she said, "Take the items you have found directly up to my room and hide them beneath my bed. Do not show them to your companions yet. There are certain things my family and I know that we cannot as yet tell you that pertain to the curse and its mystery. The only way the curse can be broken is through the unfettered courage and initiative of one important person—you. I cannot go into more details yet about the other clues or

A House

how they relate together but, as the evening passes, more will become evident to you and the facts will begin making sense."

I wanted more information. "But, Karen, I have so many more questions!"

She huffed breath out at me, a serious look on her face. "What kind of questions?"

I stopped. I didn't know if I wanted to further the conversation at that time or wait for a better time later. I looked down, my voice serious and quiet. "I want to... know more about you. I want to know more personal things about you." I looked up at her. "Is it unusual to want to know more about someone you really, really love?"

She smiled weakly as though her concerns got in the way of her feelings and she regretted it. Very gently she answered, "I'm sorry, Alex. I don't mean to sound so impersonal. I promise I'll give you all the time you need to ask me questions about anything you want, ok?"

I nodded. "Ok." I paused. "And I'll try to be a good boy and make you proud of me."

She laughed a soft little laugh. "I'm already proud of you! You're the kindest man I've ever known! I've had years to pick someone without that someone ever knowing it and you're the one! Doesn't that mean something?" She looked shyly at me. Quietly she whispered, "Doesn't that mean everything?"

We just stood and stared at each other for what seemed to be a long time before she pushed me up the stairs. "Now do as I say and I will see you in a little while in my bedroom!" As I headed up the stairs she added, "I promise."

Chapter 6
The Battle Begins

I quietly went up the stairs to the main floor and listened closely to try detecting where Adam and the old man were. Not hearing them, I closed the door behind me again and sneaked upstairs and deposited the items under the bed just as Karen had said to do. I heard talking downstairs in the library area again and started down.

It wasn't the library area at all where the voices had come from but the entrance foyer itself and the voice was that of Adam. He had discovered a suit of armor in a closet and was remarking that the weapon being held by the armor appeared to be the very one he had seen in his psychic recreation at the front door. But, before he touched it, he wanted me around in case it became a good experiment that went bad. When I showed up and he explained all this he reached in and grabbed the implement without hesitation.

Shock coursed through his face and his body slumped to the floor. He was completely unconscious and it took five minutes for him to not only regain consciousness but also cohesion. When finally his wits returned to him the guide and I began to help him to his feet. But, all the stranger, when the guide touched Adam to help him up, Adam's face contracted in great pain and shock and he again sank to the floor in unconsciousness.

A House

The old man rasped that he would go to our supplies to fetch a cool drink to help revive Adam and I assured him that would be a great idea. However, as soon as the old man had dragged his tired body out of the room Adam opened his eyes and whispered, "Is he gone?"

I whispered back in a voice frantic with worry and confusion. "Yes, he is. Adam! What is going on here?"

Adam smiled through his fear and pain. "Alex," he wheezed, "this weapon is the first item I have contacted where the murderer actually had touched it. And when the old man touched me, the energy from his body was the same energy! Alex! <u>The old man is the killer!</u>"

His statement surprised me so much I fell from my crouched position to one flat on my bottom! "Come on, Adam! How can you possibly be sure about that?"

Adam, now looking more exhausted than frightened, whispered breathlessly, "You've just got to trust me on this one, my friend! I don't know how I know what I sense, but my experiences have never lied to me in the past."

We could hear the old man returning with the water and I commented before he entered the hallway. "Adam, don't let on that you know!" I whispered. "The old man is obviously here for a reason and we'll just have to wait to find out what that reason is!"

Adam whispered back, "Maybe he figured, since this stay was sanctioned by the villagers, this would be the perfect time to recover his stolen money and leave the town without anybody ever suspecting anything."

The old man was nearly upon us. I made one last whispered statement. "Or maybe he figured he would destroy any evidence still here before we stumbled onto it!"

Adam returned quickly, "Or destroy us if we found any!"

The old man handed Adam a glass of water that Adam thanked him for most graciously. As he drank, his breathing slowed back to normal. He lay there on the floor for another ten minutes trying to rebuild his strength before attempting rising to his feet. And, as he lay there, I looked more closely at the eight-foot long spike the armor held.

Even in the dimming light of the hallway and the diminished lighting reaching inside the closet I could still make out the blood stains etched into the steel at the end of the weapon. The old man watched me intently, scowling with such intensity I felt I should have to watch my back from that time forward. In the back of my mind I kept repeating Adam's comment about the old man destroying us if we happened to discover incriminating evidence against him, which, it appeared, we had.

Adam finally figured it was safe to stand again and we sat him down in the study, only a few feet away. Yes, this was the same study I had used earlier to go all the way up to the third floor but I never indicated in the presence of the guide that I knew where the opening was to the tower or that it opened in hidden areas all the way up to the third floor.

We then knew we must force the guide into action and we began immediately tailoring our conversation to coax the man to do something to change our minds. I began, "I think it is important we attempt finding the safes hidden within the house. Don't you, Adam?"

A House

Adam knew where I was headed now. "Yes, I think that would be very important as well. If the killer did, in fact, touch the safes I might be able to get a psychic impression to that fact."

"Besides," I continued, "I was led to believe by some of the townspeople that there was a considerable sum of money left within these walls somewhere that was never found."

The guide's head snapped around toward me. "Who in the village told you that? It's a lie! Who would tell you a lie like that?"

I acted dumb. "Oh? I was told in a letter from a legal office that there was probably somewhere near a million dollars in gold and jewels still hidden within the confines of these walls."

The guide's interest peaked. "What legal office might that be?"

"Smith and somebody, I think." I could play stupid so easy. Hey, it was my nature.

"Smith and Edwards!" the guide snapped back.

"Yes, that's it. I was told there were many hiding places and safes hidden throughout the house and nobody has ever returned to find all the things left within them."

Adam played along with my game. "Do you think we can find them?"

"Yes, I think I can. You see, the valuables give off their own form of energy that can be amplified and homed in on. However, I must go up to my room and consult my psychic notebook for the right incantation to say to amplify the energies of these valuables."

A close examination of Adam's eyes would have revealed to all but the incredibly dumb that he was enjoying the game greatly. However, his voice never belied his feelings as he returned, "Well hurry up there and get the incantation! My friend and I will wait here for your speedy return!"

I made a hasty retreat out of the room and down the hall and toward the stairs saying over my shoulder, "I'll be right back."

As I hurried away I was laughing to myself. "Psychic notebook." I snickered. "Incantations." What a joke. I turned the corner at the top of the stairs, took a few steps, and entered "my" bedroom.

I immediately closed the door behind me and locked it from the inside. Before I even turned completely around in the room Karen was already laughing. "Psychic notebook with the incantation, eh?" She giggled. "What kind of idiot would believe anything like that?"

"Well this old guy has already seen Adam and I come up with some pretty unexplainable information. I figure, by now, he really doesn't have any idea of what we're doing or how we do it!" I snickered. "He knows Adam has the ability to do some pretty nifty things. By now, why wouldn't he think I have some special kind of ability as well?"

She laughed again. "Well, I'd have to agree with you about that!"

I went over to her immediately and hugged her so tightly I lifted her right off the ground. She squealed a little and planted a kiss on my neck. "I could certainly get used to having you around here all the time," she cooed in my ear.

"One promise at a time, little one. I still must fulfill the promise I made to your father and, for that, I'm

A House

afraid I could use his help in giving me inside information to help convince this guy we know where the valuables are." I paused for just a moment and looked down at her. "You three did hear Adam tell me the old man is, in fact, Elias Johnson, didn't you?"

Her head nodded rapidly. "Yes, we did. Father was nearly beside himself with rage toward the man!" Her face frowned. "I'm not sure I can control the outcome of this night any longer. This man has put all of you in terrible danger from my father and, especially, the other entities in this house. Father will do whatever is necessary to assure that man never leaves this house alive and the others will do anything they can to any of the three of you because, even if not true, they see all of you as guilty. They want to blame you for bringing the murderer back to the house to begin with."

"I understand," I said. "But I must ask your father anyway. Even if I must die, I don't care. At least I would have a greater chance of being with you forever if I died within these walls."

Without saying another word her father faded back into my view. "I understand what you need, Alex. I will go beyond what you need but you must promise me you will not reveal the details I am about to tell you to any other living soul, including your good friend, Adam. I am about to tell you the locations of all the special safes in this house and the combinations to them all."

"But, Mr. McNome. Do you think that is a good idea? To remember all the combinations I would have to write them down. To make sure I got the right combination with the right safe I would want to write down the location of the safe with the combination of it next to it." I paused for an instant. "What would happen if this information fell into the wrong hands? It would appear I betrayed you even if I weren't here."

His stern face smiled as he handed me a small bound booklet. His voice softened. "You won't have to worry about this booklet falling into the wrong hands because this is, in fact, my original notebook that I kept all my most private, valuable information within." He handed me the notebook and, as he had said, every item of significant value within the house was inventoried along with its location and the combination of the safe it was contained within.

Before I could warn him again he told me a secret: "The information you are reading is, in fact, in a secret code I developed during 'the great war' when I worked in counterintelligence. Every character you are reading is in a very intricate code not known to another living soul."

"But why does it look like plain English to me?"

"Just as you are able to see me and my family because you wish it and because we wish it, so can you read this code because you wish it and because I wish it. But I promise you none of your friends will be able to read it and any individual that might get hold of this notebook would swear up and down it is nothing but gibberish."

I ran my hand over the pages staring back at me. I wasn't really sure what to say. "Mr. McNome, I … I'm not really sure what to say. I thank you for trusting me with this incredibly valuable booklet and I promise I will not let you down."

He came close to me and put his large hands on my shoulders and patted them. "Son, I've come to feel you

A House

are the son I would have had if I had been longer on this world. I now feel very close to you for the great joy you have given my daughter in these last few hours. Even in this state we three share I at least have my wife to share my love with but my daughter has had no man to share her love with. For us, you are the only man that has treated our daughter with the love and respect we would expect a man to give her. That reason alone would normally be enough to endear you to us eternally. Having you willingly risk your life to help souls cursed to eternally roam this house only confirms our deepest feelings toward you. In my mind, I will forever be proud to say I knew such a man as you. I only wish I had known you during my lifetime. We would have become partners."

He stepped back against the windows away from me a little and as he walked backwards he continued to talk, his voice already fading away. "You are yet to face many difficulties this evening. You must face adversity of a very dangerous and serious nature. You must witness events not witnessed by any other mortals. And you must still bid farewell to my daughter who loves you so and, I know, whom you also love dearly. By morning you will feel like a war worn veteran who not only has seen the tragedies of war but has lost his family as well. And, when you succeed, as you already have indicated to us that you must, your heart may ache for awhile but you will be repaid beyond your greatest expectations."

His image was gone but a whisper of his voice remained. "Farewell, my son. I will try being ever vigil and near you this night but I must also do the task I have waited a lifetime to do to help this great evil, this great injustice, come to an end. I will be ever watchful that the other forces at work within these walls do not mistake you for the ultimate evil and bring your young life to an untimely end. Farewell ... farewell ..."

Again, Karen just stood there, staring at me. This time I just had to ask her why. "My father never approved of a single young man I showed interest in. There was always something wrong with them for one reason or another. And then you come to this house and, within a matter of minutes, my father worships the ground you walk upon." Her eyes pooled with tears again. "Never, in all my years, have I seen my father love and trust another man as much as he has with you. And in such a short period of time. It literally brings tears to my eyes!"

She tried to laugh about it as the big tears crossed those pretty cheeks again. I pulled her close to me and tried to laugh as well as I held her tightly. "And I'm going to try living up to his faith in me, as well. I will do everything within my existence to make his wishes come true." I looked down at her. Softly, I added, "As I plan on doing with you as well." I lightly kissed her for what seemed to be a long time. When we parted her face looked so soft and loving it was all I could do to leave her standing there. But I had to.

"I've got to get back downstairs right away to make our killer friend think I've got the answers to his greedy needs. I've only planned on showing where one or two of the safes are but not opening any he has never seen opened because I don't want him to observe what is inside or what the method I used to enter was."

Karen gave me one short kiss on the cheek as I turned to leave. In a very frightened, quiet voice she

A House

remarked, "Now he will want to kill you as well. He will want the book you have. He will do anything to get it."

I'd already unlocked the door but had not yet opened it. "Don't get too worried, little one. He thinks this booklet only has incantations in it that will lead me to the places. I'm not going to let him think any differently! I'll read the code that tells me the location of the safes, make up and recite an incantation, and find a safe! If he looks at the notebook and sees the code I'll just tell him it's in code so nobody else could steal the incantation."

Fear still painted itself on Karen's face. Quietly she replied, "I just hope he never saw the booklet before. If he recognized it as belonging to my father you'd be as good as dead."

I had the door open now. Quietly I replied back, "Then I just won't let him see the notebook! I'll memorize the needed information before he sees me again!"

I blew a kiss to her and her face brightened as she blew a kiss back to me. In a few moments I was back downstairs, still reading the notebook to discover the location of a few of the safes. Just as I'd suspected, a large one and a smaller one were in the library and a small one containing a large cache of diamonds and other precious jewels was in the very room Adam and the guide were still sitting in!

I had already hidden the booklet in my back pocket before I entered the room where the two men where still seated. I acted like I'd been repeating the incantation to myself over and over when I walked in.

G. Voyten

As soon as we saw each other we were all grinning toothy smiles—even the guide.

I put both arms in the air and closed my eyes. I pretended like I was in some kind of trance and loudly announced my phony incantation. "Spirits of the world! Energies of the room! Powers of this house! Guide my open arms to your most precious places! Show me your hidden gifts! Hear me spirits! Show me your wealth!"

I moaned a little bit, quite loudly, I might add, and I swayed back and forth a little bit and then, quite suddenly, I stopped abruptly and opened my eyes and smiled strangely, like under some mystical power. I shook my head a while and then walked straight over to the wall to the left of where the hidden door was. I pulled the curtain back and there, in front of us all, was a safe!

The guide was beside himself and even Adam was impressed! Of course, at that time Adam still did not know how much contact I had been having with the McNome family and I wasn't about to bring it up at that moment.

The guide wanted me to open it. I said it was not really worth opening because there was very little left in that one. In reality, that safe had the majority of all the jewels, of course, but I wanted the guide to think one of the safes with the least within it had the most just in case he slipped by us and attempted opening it.

All of a sudden I told them I was receiving more psychic information about the location of another, much larger safe. I put my arms in front of me like a divining rod and pretended to be pulled back and forth until we were standing in the library in front of a large

A House

oil painting, the wall just to the left of where the picture of Mrs. McNome hung. My arms flailed back and forth and zeroed in on that painting and then, again, my face grinned a phony smile and then I walked right over to the painting and pulled the right corner of it and it hinged away from the wall revealing another safe, probably four times larger than the first. This safe, I read, contained probably a hundred thousand dollars worth of gold at the turn of the century. Its worth at that moment was not something I wanted to waste time calculating.

Again I commented that I detected the safe contained only some low value bonds and stocks from the old days, most of which were from companies long since gone broke.

One more, I thought. Mr. McNome had a safe in that same room that was probably the one the killer had robbed in the first place and knew the location of. I went into my swoon once again and, this time, walked directly over to the right wall, the same wall as the portrait of Mrs. McNome, and, just to the right of her portrait, pulled another oil painting away from the wall to reveal its hidden location. Since I knew this was the one that had already been ransacked, I decided it was the one to open.

This was the only safe whose combination I had memorized before returning to the company of my companions. I walked to the safe and, without hesitation, dialed the combination and let the door swing back widely.

To my utter amazement the contents of the safe was not what I had expected! According to what impressions I had gotten about this safe being the one robbed of many thousands of dollars and securities, the contents appeared to have been returned, save the few thousands of dollars I had hidden upstairs under Karen's bed!

I could hear the sounds of awe coming from behind me. I think Adam was in awe and the guide was in shock! I could say nothing now because I was so unprepared for what I saw I could no longer play the game.

Before anyone could say a word I slammed the safe shut and spun the combination lock on the door. A protest immediately burst out from both men staring at me in disbelief! They, of course, wanted to know what made me close the door. "Fear," I assured them. "The psychic force whispered to me that whosoever took from that safe would not live to see morning."

Adam almost blew the game when he blurted out, "Well I was listening to psychic forces and I didn't hear any telling you that!"

The guide, however, didn't say another word. He just stared at the safe with a mean, hungry look in those tired old eyes. While he was still staring at it I repeated myself: "I said whoever removes the contents of this safe will probably die before morning! Adam, the psychic forces don't lie!"

By now I was staring deep into Adam's eyes. All of a sudden he understood and backed down. "Ok, ok, I hear you! If the psychic forces tell you don't touch the stuff we don't touch the stuff." Under his voice, though, he added, "But it sure would have been nice!"

Darkness had closed in around the house. Stillness hung like death over everything. A flash of lightening in the distance came through the windows of the

A House

library and, a few moments later, the ominous rumble of thunder shook the room. Although it did not unnerve the guide, Adam and I both stopped in mid stride and drew our complete attention outside. Almost in a mumble Adam said exactly what I had thought: "Funny, there was not supposed to be a storm in this area tonight."

The guide was anxious for me to find more hidden treasures for him but my interests turned away from treasures and toward the changing characteristics of the house—the very room we were in. I hadn't seen a phenomenon like the one I had just then noticed since I was a young child toying with the concepts of ghosts and learned about "good white ghosts" and "bad black ghosts" and, even at that, doubted what I'd been told. Although the guide was impatient with me, Adam saw the concern on my face and decided to follow my eyes to the object of my concern.

Quietly he replied, "I see it, I see it." And then another. And another. And another. Soon the room had blackened unnaturally in every corner except the one we had been standing in and more blackness grew from the little areas of black we'd first observed.

Eventually the guide stopped in mid sentence of complaint and looked around the room and noticed the unusual black shapes in each of the corners and how the shapes seemed to grow taller and wider as we watched.

He turned to me to ask what it was. "Have you ever really seen a ghost before?" I asked.

"No. I don't believe there is such a thing as a ghost," he answered.

Without removing my eyes from the shapes around the room I replied, "Well, I never believed in them, either, but I think, if you look around, you'll experience your first encounter with quite a few of them."

Another bright flash of lightening hit somewhere outside and, moments later again, the pounding roll of the thunder shook the room. I remarked, "Did you notice that, when the lightening literally illuminated the entire room like daylight, the dark patches around the corners of the room remained dark?"

Now I had the guide's attention. In a voice as dry as paper he whispered, "Yes. Yes, I noticed."

I put the picture back in place over the safe and slowly inched my way out of the room. The others wisely followed. Physically shaking, I made my way out of the library but did take the time to look back into the room once more as a flash of lightening again lit the room. The shapes were now life-sized and walking away from the corners of the room and toward us, very, very slowly. I whispered, "I think it would be an excellent time to retire to our rooms upstairs and act like we're not really interested in the treasures of these safes right now."

We proceeded upstairs at somewhat of an above-normal pace; all a little unnerved by the experience we'd just been through. I convinced the others to come into my room for a few minutes so we could discuss what, if anything, we should do during the remainder of the evening. Quite understandably, the consensus was we should do nothing for the remainder of the night, unless you might want to call "staying alive" something.

A House

Within moments after our decision the old guide excused himself and said he must rush to his room and make his preparations for sleeping. Adam and I wished him a good night and the next sounds we heard were the slamming and dead-bolting of his door.

Adam and I were finally alone. I could begin explaining all the fantastic things that had happened while I had been out of his sight. Likewise, Adam had things he wanted to tell me as well.

I began by telling him about Karen and her family. He doubted me but tried to believe. I so wanted him to see Karen. I asked him if he would believe what he saw if I let him. He said that sounded rather strange coming from me to him because, ever since we'd known each other, he'd been telling me things that were happening that I could only take on faith. So I decided to introduce him to Karen.

I called for Karen to enter the room. I called her time after time and, finally, told her not to be afraid of Adam because he was like my brother in closeness and trustworthiness.

The solitary candle in the room dimmed to where the room was dimly illuminated and Karen faded into view sitting right beside me. The look on Adam's face was unbelievable! He was in utter shock!

"How did you do that?" he gasped.

Karen answered, "I was here all the time. I was just afraid to show myself to anyone other than Alex."

The dumb look of amazement had not left his face but he stupidly replied, "Actually, I was talking to Alex but your answer was … <u>better!</u>"

Karen smiled brightly and her eyes danced in the light from the candle. The room lightened and we could see her much better. But the look on her face changed to one of concern and fear. She turned to me and continued. "Alex, the mood of the house is changing rapidly. The next few hours will be very dangerous for you and your friend. I strongly suggest you both stay in here with me to protect you because the others are active and very, very angry right now." She looked directly into my eyes. "They know now that the old man is the murderer and they want to take revenge against him! They all do, including my father!"

A flash of lightening and an almost immediate blasting clap of thunder startled us all for a moment. I asked, "But what can we do at this time of the night? Are these others going to come upstairs and drag us from our beds for revenge?"

She shook her head. "No, they will pass by this room because I am in here with you and my mother roams the halls reassuring the others you are not a threat." She smiled a little. "She's actually telling quite a few of the nicer ones that there is a very good chance you and Adam can help them to their eternal peace, like you did for that nice man in the tunnel today."

Adam interrupted. "What others? What nice man in the tunnel?" He paused only a moment. "And when did you meet her mother?"

Karen smiled. "And father."

Adam, still wearing a shocked, stupid look on his disbelieving face, asked, "And father?"

I laughed. "Where did you think I got the locations of those safes? And how did you think I knew the combination to that safe in the library? You really didn't believe in my psychic incantations, did you?"

A House

He shook his head and still looked puzzled. "Well, it sure sounded like garbage to me and even looked like garbage to me. Until you found the first safe without even hesitating! Just how did you do it?"

I chuckled. "Brian McNome, Karen's dad, gave me a secret booklet of his that details every location, every combination, every item, every place in the house." I showed it to him forgetting it was encrypted.

He looked at it curiously. "And you can understand this junk?"

I snickered. "Mr. McNome gave me the ability to see this code as though it were plain English! All I had to do was read a few of them before I entered the room, memorize one combination, and come up with some fake magic words to mutter at the bone head."

Now Adam was grinning. He grinned as he looked at me, then at Karen, and then back at me. He whispered, "Well I'll be darned!"

And then Adam looked long and seriously at Karen. "Karen McNome, I must say you are absolutely the most beautiful young lady I have ever had the pleasure to know." He just stared at her. In almost a whisper he added, "Stunning. You are absolutely breathtaking!"

Karen blushed. She turned her head away, grinning ear to ear. Very quietly she answered, "Where were you young men when I was at a courting age?" She giggled.

I hated to be the honest one but I answered, "When you were at a courting age Adam and I weren't even born!" I looked at her to see if I'd hurt her feelings. I hastily continued, "I didn't mean to hurt your feelings, ma'am."

She looked at me, still grinning. "Ma'am," she snickered and rolled her eyes back. "Nobody ever called me 'ma'am'!" She chuckled to herself.

Just then she snapped her head sideways a bit as though listening. Adam and I remained silent. She listened intently for a while before commenting. "Father is about to do a bad thing. He is going to begin working on Mr. Johnson to subconsciously convince him to return downstairs to the library to steal the contents of that safe he knows how to open." She looked at me. "That was the one he had originally stolen the money from, you probably remember."

I nodded. And then I asked. "Did it catch you off guard to see so much money in that safe? If he had stolen the money, then why did the safe still look full?"

She paled. "That even caught Father off guard! It should have been nearly empty based on the amount of money Mother originally found in his toolbox! The only thing Father could think of was due to the little money you and I found today the remainder of what was taken was placed back in the safe for safekeeping! Who would have guessed the robber would have returned the money to the safe!"

Adam interjected, "Money? What money?"

Without even batting an eye Karen replied, "The money we found in the room of absolute evil."

Adam was looking from Karen to me for additional information. I added, "We met down in the basement today and Karen convinced me to check out the tunnel that leads off the property. We discovered an old man who had frozen to death in the tunnel first and, later, a room used for storing garden implements that our killer had used to cut up the family and discard off the

A House

property at an area just beyond the end of the tunnel." I paused and looked deep into Adam's eyes. "Adam, being an empath, the place could kill you. Seriously."

Karen continued. "The evil in that room was so strong it nearly killed Alex before we discovered the clues hidden there and made our escape."

I continued. "When we got to the end of the tunnel and looked in the toolbox Karen assured me the quantity of money in the toolbox was not great enough to represent what had been taken."

Karen finished the story with these words. "But the murder weapon used on my mother was in the bottom of the toolbox."

A troubled look covered Adam's face. "But what about these 'others' you've both mentioned."

Karen explained, "There is a graveyard on the property dating from the Civil War. Many of the men buried there still spiritually roam these halls. And they are not nice men."

Chapter 7
The Lull Before the Storm

*T*he storm subsided and the moon came out. Adam moved to the window and said it seemed to be a more tranquil time all of a sudden. Karen looked away for a moment and said, "Something is up. I must go and check." In an instant she was gone.

I smiled at Adam. "What do you think of her?"

His eyes grew large and a toothy grin smeared across his face. "What do you want me to think of her? She's a dead girl!"

It took me by surprise and was a little disappointing. Adam saw I was not taking this lightly and corrected himself. "Alex, she is truly one of the most beautiful women I have ever seen, alive or dead, but, bottom line is, she's dead! Chances are, after tonight, you'll never see her again!"

Very quietly I replied, "I know." I looked up into his face. "But I'll always love her, Adam. I know that sounds stupid, seeing as how I only met her a few hours ago, but I've never known a woman that actually loved me without me having to go out of my way to make her happy."

Adam interjected, "Yeah, sure! You've come to her house where her soul is eternally cursed, you've returned the man here that killed her entire family, you've given her father the perfect opportunity to get revenge on this guy for sixty years of bad news, you've

A House

very likely brought enough details together to remove the curse from them all, and yet you don't feel you've done anything special for them!"

I frowned at him. "ADAM! I WOULD HAVE DONE THAT ANYWAY!"

He grinned ear to sickening ear. In almost a whisper he answered, "Yeah, I know! That's what's so funny! They think you're great because you're … great!!"

Well, that sure blew my argument that was to follow! I calmed down and quietly answered, "Thanks."

Karen appeared beside me again and immediately began talking. "My father says the guide was too disturbed by the storm and the images of the others downstairs to be convinced to leave his room. So they're all backing off until the man changes his mind."

"And how long will that last?" I asked.

"Hours. Possibly all night. The others are listening to my father since this is his night and his chance to break his bonds. They have all settled down and do not represent a threat to any of you right now."

Alex released a long breath of relief. "I think I'll go over to my room, then, and try to get some rest!"

I smiled at him. I paused. "Thanks, Adam. Thanks for being such a great friend."

He smiled back. "I was going to say the same to you, my friend!" He looked at Karen sitting so quiet and proper next to me. His face softened. He moved to her and took both her hands in his. She stood. "Karen, I cannot possibly tell you how much I appreciate meeting you this evening! You are a magnificent woman and you will never, ever know what a positive impression you have made on me and my very best friend in my life." He kissed her hands and squeezed them. "I thank you from the bottom of my heart for allowing yourself to enter into <u>my</u> life." He looked at me. "And especially into the life of my dear, lonely friend here."

He kissed her cheek, unlocked my door, waved back at us, and left the room to go to his own. In a moment we heard his door shut and lock.

When my attention turned back toward Karen she was, again, staring at me, not the door. I had seen a look such as was in her eyes in other women's eyes before—but never while they were looking at me, only others. The look in her eyes was a look I had waited all my life to see in the eyes of a woman and never had experienced. I was not sure what to make of it and I doubted what the next step should be.

Karen, however, knew exactly what she wanted and proceeded to pursue such. She sat on the bed, turning her head slightly sideways and looking up at me so that her eyes looked especially large, bright, and deep blue. All I could do was weakly smile at her. After all, I was never very good with women, why should I suddenly be better? Luckily for me she detected my hesitation and gently drew me into her confidence.

"I want to know you very well, Alex. I want us to become very close, intimate friends this night."

My eyes would not look into hers. I looked down toward my knees. Quietly answered, "I know you do, Karen." I paused. "And I would like to get to know you better as well."

A House

My heart was breaking. I wanted so much to tell her everything in the world. I wanted her to know how much I cared for her, how much I wanted to be with her, how much I appreciated her, how much I even appreciated how much she felt for me, like no woman before ever could. But I was afraid. I felt I would burst forth like a young child and the fear of rejection loomed before me like a gallows.

My eyes, when I finally looked into hers with my pleading, futile glance, must have spoken for themselves for she answered my unspoken words just as though all had been said. "I know what is going through your mind right now. Fear. Hope. Isolation. Doubt. These are the thoughts running wild through my mind as well. It is not that I can actually see your thoughts, although I can feel your spirit without you knowing it. But the look in your eyes matches the feeling within my heart so I know we are both having the same doubts and fears and questions."

She took my right hand between both her hands and rested her hands on her lap. Her top hand stroked the back of mine and her bottom hand squeezed. "Dear Alex. I know the fear running fastest through both our minds is how to live a lifetime of thoughts and love in just the few hours we shall have together. My strongest impression is how we both want to be as close to an earthly body as is emotionally possible right now, tonight, because, in both of our lives, we never before have experienced another to care that much for us." She sighed one long, sad sigh. "Somehow, in what seemed to be just an instant in time, our spirits have met and melded. Our hearts have become one. I cannot tell you I understand all that has happened or even why it has been allowed to happen. I can only tell you for me this is the last chance I will ever have to be loved by a man for all eternity. When the morning comes I surely will be gone to wherever my freed spirit will be allowed to rest and I know you will not arrive at this same resting place for many years yet to come. So, somehow, I must find a way the two of us can feel as though we know each other in the most personal of ways. I must find a way to allow you into my life the way I have been able to see into yours without you ever knowing it. I must find a way to let you feel as comfortable with me as I feel in my heart with you." She paused and looked sheepishly at me. "Does this make sense to you?"

She looked down at her lap then and squeezed my hand between both her hands. In almost a whisper she continued. "I will understand if you take on a wife soon in your life and I would never ask you not to do this. I know it is possible to love many, not just one, and I would not expect you to be lonely the remaining years of your life." She looked deep into my eyes with a look that said she knew something about me I didn't know about myself again and she added, "And I know you will find another that you will love just as deeply as we love each other right now."

This time I squeezed her hand. "I have never found one woman to love me in all my years. What would make you think, after finding you, I could possibly find another?"

She looked up at me and tried to smile but a tear running down her cheek said what her lips could not. Again, she looked down at our intermingled hands. "I ... know you will find another." She looked into my eyes, tears pooling and then running from her own. "I even know who this other woman is." She again smiled through her tears. "And I want you to love her, just as you love me. It is so very important that you do."

I couldn't say another word. My emotions were getting the best of me. I put both arms around her and pulled her close to me and, in an instant, she put both arms around me as well and our bodies once again molded to each other like they were never meant to be apart.

I sighed. "But there are still a million questions to ask, a million feelings to experience. I want to know you the way you have come to know me, even though I was never conscious of it."

We sat very close to each other. It was then I noticed probably the only "strange" or "unusual" condition of her existence next to me: she did not give off heat where we touched. Even holding her hands, my hands never warmed to her touch. It was like touching flesh but holding air. I could feel the texture of her clothes, the softness and sweet smell of her hair, see the sparkle in her eyes, but not feel the warmth of her body. It was not like touching cold flesh but like touching air itself.

I really had so many things going through my mind I didn't know what to ask first. I wanted to know what it was like being in the state she was in but, even though the questions were so technically intriguing, personal questions seemed so much more important. What were her interests? What were her loves, her hates, her fears? What would she want more than anything else in the world? Of course, I could not ask,

"What do you want more than anything else in life?" because life had nothing to do with it. But, thinking over the concept, I figured phrasing things carefully was like watching commonly used phrases around individuals with obvious conditions. It would be like saying, "I can't see you doing that," to a blind person.

So I asked her to tell me about her life and what she'd enjoyed, feared, and regretted.

"My life was a very good one with much love from my parents, although I know there was much resentment from the community because we were wealthy and they were not. For that reason I had no friends from the town, only from the schools I'd attended when sent away for an education. It was not that Father resented or disliked the townspeople or thought the local school system was not good, but that the other children and many of the parents mistreated me and would not accept me into the community."

"Who was your best friend?" I asked.

She smiled and was looking like her mind was a million miles away. "Little Marianne McGreggor: a spirited red-haired girl with a temper as hot as her shocking red hair and the cunning of a fox." She laughed out loud. "Little Marianne and I had many a grand time teasing the other girls in school and playing tricks on the teachers!"

Smiling as well I asked, "And what became of Marianne?"

Karen's face went from absolute happiness to absolute sadness in an instant. "Marianne was killed in a traffic accident one night on her way home from another friend's house. I never got to see her again,

A House

even in death." She sighed. "Maybe, if the curse is broken, I'll be able to see Marianne again."

My face saddened. I paused. Softly, I asked, "How old was she?"

"Thirteen," she said, looking down at her hands.

"Oh." I paused again and could hear the wind hissing through the trees outside. I tried to lift my voice. "Did you have any other friends as good as Marianne later in life?"

She smiled. "No, never another as dear to me as little Marianne. But there was Katie Fuller that was my next best friend. We were friends through the remainder of school and even went to college together."

I tried to smile. "What about boys? Did you have any boyfriends?"

She was smiling and shaking her head. "Yes, there were a few boys." She looked up at me. "But never any like you."

I didn't understand. "What do you mean?"

She sighed. "I always had two problems: I was rich and I was, shall we say, 'pleasing to the eye of the opposite sex.' Between those two conditions I was always a challenge to some boy or, later, some man. I was never just 'Karen McNome, the yellow-haired dreamer', the way my father referred to me. No, to these men I was always 'Karen McNome, the rich girl' or 'Karen McNome, the beautiful challenge'." She looked sadly into my eyes. She took my hand and held it against her heart. Her eyes softened. "They were never interested in what was in here. They were interested in 'a catch'." She smiled at me tenderly. "Do you realize no man I ever dated ever asked me what I thought about anything? No man before you, that is. I was treated as though I were a trophy being carried around to exhibit to the other men. No, I was not the prize, what I <u>was</u> was the prize."

I was shaking my head and I let my hand caress her face. "But, Karen, why would anybody want to do that to you? You're beautiful from the inside out! It wouldn't have mattered if you were physically beautiful or rich or anything else! Beauty starts from the inside and works its way to the surface. I've known many physically beautiful women that were only beautiful on the surface. They loved themselves more than anything else in the world and put no value in life greater than their own! But you must realize people like you are the exception, not the rule. Most rich, beautiful women love what they are more than <u>who</u> they are."

She smiled weakly and paused before asking, "And what did you like the most about me?"

I smiled back broadly. "I immediately appreciated the fact you cared so much for me without even knowing me! Standing there in the dark with you on one side of the room and me on the other I was impressed how you could care for me but still want to protect me from the truth."

She smiled shyly. "And you cared for me right away? Even though you could not see what I looked like?"

I smiled back softly. "I cared deeply for you because I liked you from the inside first. The outside was just frosting on the cake!"

A House

She smiled but turned her face away from me. Carefully, she asked, "Would you love me if I were not so attractive?"

I put my arm around her and drew her very close. I nestled my head in her hair and kissed her cheek. "The women in my past that I loved the most were not the greatest beauties. Some were, shall we say, a little less than 'common'? But each I've loved the very most shared one characteristic: their softness and generosity of the soul."

Without turning to look at me I noticed her face had a concerned expression. "Do you have someone you … love right now?"

Without hesitating I replied, "Of course I do!"

She jerked and slowly, sadly turned her head toward me. Quietly, she said, "Who?"

I grinned. "<u>You</u>, of course! I love you right now!"

She laughed and hugged me. "I'm sorry! I forgot you might be referring to me!" She rolled her eyes in her head and repeated, "I mean, do you love anyone other than me? A female? Not a relative? Someone you might consider marrying?"

I calmed down a little. "No," I said quietly. "No woman wanted to put up with me. The best of the best of my female friends are married to the best of the best of my male friends. The other women in my life still see themselves as the most important events in their lives."

She sighed. "Tell me a bit of your past, your childhood."

"Well, I can't use the excuse of being rich or being beautiful for having problems fitting in throughout my childhood. I'm not beautiful or even particularly attractive. My family was dirt poor when I was young and it was practically a daily embarrassment just going to school in clothes that were torn and worn out. I was teased about my clothes, my looks, and even where my family lived. To make it worse, I was always smarter than the other children in my classes and they harassed me constantly because I could not fit in. I was more interested in science and mathematics than sports and girls. I wanted to write poetry, not go on a date. Even in college the other men would not include me in their activities. They wanted to go drinking. I wanted to study astronomy and physics. They wanted to go dating. I had to work after classes to pay my way through college. We had nothing in common."

"But ... Adam?"

"I didn't meet Adam until years after I'd started my own business. By the time I'd completed college I was already working for a major business and getting experience in how to handle marketing and finance and shipping. I could see a thousand ways of making the business run more efficiently and I pleaded with the management to allow me to help. They laughed. What could a college brat know about their business, they wanted to know? No, they'd been in the business a lifetime and knew everything there was to know about the business. So, with five thousand dollars I'd saved for three years of work after college, I started my own business. A year later the company I'd worked for before went broke and the workers there came to work for me. But not the managers or administrators, of course. They already knew too much about the business to listen to an upstart like me."

Her face saddened. "No girls in your life?"

A House

I sighed. "Yes, there were girls. In school and college I was used, occasionally, because they needed help with their homework or they needed someone to pay their way to an event. Yes, they all thought I was such a nice guy. But, when it came down to the wire, they never had time for me, only the other guys. Even when I had a business and was successful the only women interested in me were the ones that wanted to use me to make them rich at my expense or the ones that wanted to get the men they claimed to care for a job at big money working for me. No, no woman ever loved me for me." I looked at her. "Sound familiar?"

She sighed and nodded her head, looking down and away from me. In a voice as soft as a whisper she muttered, "Two lonely people meeting to comfort each other at last."

I squeezed her close to me and kissed her forehead. "Yes, two lonely people who need each other."

I tried to change the mood slightly. "But tell me some of the things that are important to you." I paused. "And why were you attracted to me?"

She laid her head on my shoulder and I felt her arm wind around my back. "I always wanted a man that could love me for who I am inside, who would think of me as the most important part of his life. I wanted a man that thought the most important thing he could give me was ... his time and company. Someone that thought an exciting evening would be sitting around the fireplace with a bowl of popped corn, snuggling up together, whispering tender little thoughts in my ear, holding me close, like we are, talking about emotional issues, like we are, caring about feeling good about each other..." She turned and looked at me with a knowing look on her face. "... Like we are!" She grinned. "What do you know? Except for the popped corn and the fireplace, I have just what I've always dreamed of having!" She grinned even wider. "I have you!"

I thought I'd tease her just a bit. "You don't think I'm actually just interested in how you look or the chance I might get some money out of this deal?"

She looked at me scornfully. "Of course not! You treated me well before you knew what I looked like and it would be pretty difficult for me to 'give in' to giving you money! Besides, as you've already explained, you're well off in your own right!"

I squeezed her tightly and laughed. "That's a pretty brave statement coming from a woman that never found the right man before!"

Her face was still stern. "And that's a pretty foolish statement coming from a man that never found the right woman, either!"

I looked at her, she looked at me, and we both laughed out loud. Her face softened and her voice was as gentle as her skin was smooth. "But I think we've both made a wise choice. I know tonight will be our only night, but we must enjoy the sheer pleasure of each other for tonight."

I kicked off my shoes, tried to smile, and bounced over on the bed until I was lying down. She looked down at me, still not appearing any too happy. I put my arms out toward her. She smiled and curled up next to me on the bed and sighed again.

The evening went just that way for nearly an hour. We just laid like that, holding each other, listening to the gentle wind blowing through the trees just beyond

A House

the window. I stroked her hair and nestled my face close to hers and not a word was spoken.

I was feeling quite contented and nearly fell asleep. How I could feel like this was some kind of a natural act I should be doing I could not understand and yet it felt like something I wanted to always be able to do. And then Karen scooted up a little and kissed me tenderly. She turned her body so it lay atop mine and both my arms wrapped around her as I stroked her hair. The kiss started as an emotional, affectionate kiss but continued into one of growing feelings, of passion. And when we parted from the kiss she whispered, "There is more to caring than just holding each other, you know."

I stroked the hair back from her face and smiled. "Karen, are you telling me you want to do things a little more physical in nature?"

She smiled back. "Alex, am I ever going to get another chance?"

I lifted my head toward hers and kissed her softly. "You know, maybe we shouldn't remove the family curse and then you wouldn't have to go on to wherever you're going to go on to."

She frowned. "But you still don't know how terrible it is to relive your death every night! Each of us in this house must reenact our deaths every night at a different time after midnight!"

My face sobered, my voice softened. "Oh. Oh, Karen, I'm so sorry! I didn't know that!"

She continued. "Your friend, Adam, has experienced the intensity of the deaths of my parents today. He physically felt the pain of death, the fear of death, even the dying of death." She paused. "Each of us experiences the same each night, every night. Each of us relives the curse of the death, the pain of the death."

I brought my fingers to her lips. "Enough. You've said more than enough. I think we should keep our minds on each other the remainder of the hours we have together and think of the breaking of the curse as the rest you and your parents deserve."

She smiled again and we kissed tenderly. My hands went to the back of her dress and began opening the clasps that had held it together. In a whisper I asked, "But what if your parents are watching?"

Her eyes looked soft and dreamy. Gently she answered, "My parents approve of my activities and they are too busy watching another within the house to impose upon my privacy."

She sat up on her knees and reached behind her and gently, in one motion, let the top of her dress fall away from her shoulders and down to her waist. In the candlelight I could still plainly see the contour of her chest rising and falling above the lacy undergarment straining to contain her. She got up from the bed and allowed her dress to slip to the floor in one quick movement and then, one strap at a time, allowed her slip to fall away as well. Her eyes never leaving my face, she proceeded to remove her stockings, slowly, rolling each down past her thighs before pulling them from her feet and placing them each on the chair beside the bed. She returned next to me on the bed and reached behind her back and began undoing the laces. Soon she took my hands and guided them behind her and I continued to undo her remaining clothing, slowly removing each item while she kissed me repeatedly,

A House

each kiss more intense and sensual than the one before. In a whisper she concluded, "Now let's pass this evening as though it were the last evening we should ever have upon earth together." She kissed me passionately and we tightly embraced. I allowed the natural things to happen and tried not to think of never being with her again to repeat the events of the night.

Our interlude lasted a most enjoyable period of time until the gentle hushing of the wind outside and the bed inside was broken by screaming and yelling downstairs followed by a bone crushing "thud" and a screaming, gurgling conclusion. Karen sat up in bed as though the devil himself had entered the room to steal her soul. In a frantic raspy whisper she said, "That was mother reenacting her death in the library!"

Of course, I was already sitting straight up in bed as well, my eyes as big as saucers, asking, "Is there anything I can do?"

Her body slumped and she looked down at the bed. "No. That is just the horror we must face every night. First it is Mother, two hours later, near four in the morning it is Father, and then, at dawn, it is I." She looked at me, tears streaming down her face, frustration burning in her eyes. "That is why everything is so terrible! I cannot take the pain of us facing death every night for the rest of eternity and yet, if the curse is broken, I will never see you again!"

I held her close again. "We must break the curse! We must accept the fact that this night is the only night of love we will ever have, make the most of it, and let the curse be broken!"

Karen had lain back down and I was about to when Adam and the guide were up and at my door. Adam stepped inside but could not see Karen, although she was still plainly visible to me. Adam, with his eyes glowing at me through the darkness, was straining to whisper, "Did you hear that? Did you hear that? It sounded like a scream from downstairs!"

I tried to whisper back to both of them. "Yes, it was the reenactment of Sarah McNome's death downstairs. Each night, at different times, each of those killed within this house must go through their deaths again." I laid back down turning my back to Adam and the guide and toward Karen. "But nothing else is going to happen for hours so go get some sleep." I didn't want to mention Karen in front of the guide so I just added, "The ghosts only haunt the first floor, I guess, so we should be safe here on the second."

I could hear Adam mumbling, "Oh, ok, I guess," and closing the door behind him as he left. I turned over just to verify that they had left, and then turned back away from the door.

Karen, still under the covers, still naked, still smiling, giggled. I smiled back. She whispered, "There is no reason not to continue taking advantage of this night, is there?"

I grinned and pulled her over me. "Not a single reason that I can think of." I assured her.

She grinned back. "So just where were we?"

Chapter 8
The Battle Continues

I woke two hours later to the sound of wind whipping up against the glass and an ear piercing scream from downstairs. Karen and I both sat up in bed again. This time I commented, "Your dad reenacting his death, right?" She only nodded her head. A look of fear and anguish was etched deeply on her face.

Again, Adam and the guide stumbled, fumbled, and appeared in my room. Again, they could not see Karen. Adam's eyes were, again, as large as saucers, and this time he insisted we at least check out the downstairs for what was going on. "I'd feel much better to assure myself there is nobody else in this house of a physical nature to kill us in our sleep than just assume there really is such a thing as a ghost reliving a death scene!"

I got up immediately, threw on my clothes, and we all rushed downstairs to the entrance and the front door, Karen calling to me, trying to convince me it was not a good thing to try to do. Even with only the three candles we carried with us I could see something different with the front door long before we'd reached it. The long ago faded bloodstain which had run from the cut on the door to the puddle stain on the floor looked somehow darker. And, as we reached the door, we discovered why: "This is real blood on the door and the floor!" Adam shouted. "The blood from the original murder has somehow returned!"

The house began taking on a different characteristic again. Adam had not even completed his last words when the winds outside intensified and blew in great, massive bursts against the house and the entire foyer grew noticeably darker, in spite of our three candles remaining lighted. A dark, ominous groan seemed to grow from the walls themselves and echoed throughout the downstairs area. It grew louder and louder and the room grew colder.

The guide bolted for the door to escape. "Let's get out of here!" he screamed. But the door would not open. He yelled and pounded on the door before he was suddenly thrown clear across the foyer and slid across the floor to the staircase.

He slowly picked his old body up and screamed, "We must get away! We must try escaping upstairs!"

His candle gone somewhere else down the hallway, we could just barely make out his form in the distant darkness as he attempted hobbling up the stairs as fast and his ancient legs would take him.

He abruptly stopped about a quarter of the way up the steps as we hurried to follow his lead when he was very forcefully thrown up against the wall as though being held by the neck by some unseen force. We could hear him choking as he sputtered and gagged and, somehow, began sliding up the wall, repeating over and over, "I didn't do it! I didn't do it!"

A cold breeze blowing within the house extinguished the candles Adam and I were carrying. We would have been completely sightless if not for frequent bright lightening flashes tearing in through the

A House

windows around us. It felt like icy hands were now grabbing at me, touching me, trying to hold me back. I could not tell if their attempts were to keep me from saving the old man's life or detaining me to wait my turn to be strangled to death as well.

Adam was yelling, "I can't move! I can't get to the old man! Something is holding me back! I can't move! Alex, what are we going to do?"

I yelled back above the moaning that was now competing in volume with the thunder booming all around us outside. "Keep trying, Adam! We've got to get away from this area! We've got to get upstairs!" I was making slow progress toward the old man even though the cold hands on my bare arms now felt like the intensity was cutting my skin and my feet felt like they were walking upstream in a very fast moving river. "We've got to get the old man away from here right now!"

The old man appeared nearly dead by the time we'd reached him, still struggling against the wall. His eyes were rolling up in his head and a small trickle of blood was coming from his mouth. His only movements were a few slight jerks to his arms and legs as his body made its final struggles to survive. But the moment I managed to touch his arm it all instantly stopped! The storm had subsided, the moaning had ceased, the darkness in the room had gone, the struggling with unseen forces had left! It was as though it had never happened! The only way I felt it all had truly taken place was from the old man, falling to the steps, grabbing his throat, wheezing for each breath, and the cold feeling of blood running down my arms from where someone or something had been detaining me so forcibly.

I looked at Adam. I whispered, "Is it over?"

Even in the dark I could see the terror on Adam's face. "No, it is not over. It is only the end of one battle in the war."

He looked around the room like there were things to be seen I could not see. Fear still etched into his face, he continued. "Can you hear them whispering?" I shook my head. His face also showed confusion and agitation. "Too many voices at one time!" he loudly, hoarsely whispered. "But I can hear them say things like, 'They will never leave us', and 'It is not over', and 'The old man must die.'"

The old man was just regaining consciousness and his breathing began to recover from the raspy sound of before. When he recovered from his encounter the first thought on his mind was escape. Before Adam and I could stop him he shouted, "I must get out of here!" and he bolted for the front door again. And, as before, he no sooner touched the front door than he was instantly and violently thrown back across the room to the foot of the stairs. A loud moan echoed through the house at the moment the old man touched the front door and the last sounds of it faded at the same time as those of his impact with the marble floor. Fading with the echoes of the attack was the sound of evil laughter.

By that time Adam and I were at the foot of the stairs and helped the old man back to his feet. Without hesitation we headed back up the stairs to the false safety of our rooms. As we helped the old man up the stairs Adam whispered, "I get the impression the evil

A House

will not come up to the bedroom level to attack us. They want us to come to them first."

The old man shook violently as we helped him up the stairs and to his room. His legs would not bear his weight and dragged weakly as we assisted him beneath each arm. But he had recovered fairly well by the time we had arrived at his room.

I sat him on his bed and Adam disappeared to his room for a moment and was back in a flash with a flask of whisky. He weakly smiled and said, "I always carry a flask as a bracer just in case I have a weak moment." He looked into my eyes. "And this evening I think we could all use a little encouragement!"

We took turns choking down encouragement from Adam's confidence builder and, in a relatively short period of time, even the guide felt confident enough to attempt falling back to sleep.

Adam and I returned to my room. I closed the door behind him. In a voice quiet enough not to be heard by anyone else I whispered, "That was a close one, Adam. I don't think we're going to get out of here tonight."

Adam had quite a story to tell me. It seems he'd finally been able to sort out enough of the voices he'd heard to get the idea of what was going on. "They mean to kill the guide tonight. They don't especially want to harm the two of us, but the impression I got was that the guide would never live to see another sunrise."

I questioned, "And the events downstairs?"

"They were holding us back so Mr. McNome would be able to strangle the guide. There were many voices during the attack and I got the impression they were talking directly to the guide. The strongest voice was saying things like 'assassin' and 'murderer.'" Adam's face blanked of all expression and his eyes were locked on mine. "They feel the guide will attempt to rob the house again to reclaim the money. They feel that nobody—including you and I—can leave this house with one dollar of the money hidden within this house."

In a dark corner of the room Karen dimly appeared, sitting on the chair where earlier she had deposited her clothing, although at this time she was completely dressed once again. As though she had been a part of the entire conversation she interjected, "It is just as I had said earlier. My father wants to see the estate go to our only living relative. And he wants this relative to restore this house to its previous glory. And he wants revenge against the murderer of our family. And he will not allow any of you to leave until his revenge this night is complete."

Both of us were startled by her appearance. We snapped around toward her and tried to calm down a little. I asked, "Was your father angry with us when we attempted to stop him from killing the guide?"

She smiled. "Of course not! He realizes you only attempted to do what you thought best! That is why neither of you was allowed to be injured and why the attack toward the murderer stopped the instant you touched him. Father did not want you harmed." She paused. Quietly, she continued, "He ... loves you like a son."

Adam shook his head. "This is truly strange!" He looked at me, his face part smile, part fear, part confusion. "We're only here a few hours and you've got a girl that's loved you all your life that you've

A House

never seen before and a man considering you as a long, lost member of his family that you've never met!"

I opened my mouth to speak but Karen spoke first. "What makes you think we have never met Alex before?" She smiled a knowing, cunning smile. "What makes you think my father does not know everything there is to know about Alex?"

Even I had a difficult time with that. I answered. "Even I don't know everything about myself. How could your father? Does he know I was orphaned at two years old and was raised by a family that had found me next to my dead family in a camping accident? Does he know I don't even know my real last name because there was not enough left of my family to even recognize who they were?"

Karen, still smiling gently, answered, "He knows more than that." Her eyes sparkled and her face grinned. As she faded into the darkness her words faded into the walls. "He knew your father. And your grandfather. And your great-grandfather." Karen had faded into the dirty room as though she'd never been there and Adam and I still stared at the area where she'd been, still not speaking. Finally, shaking his head and standing to leave, Adam concluded, "This is too weird! How could a ghost in a house we've never been in before know more about our pasts than we know about them ourselves?"

I shook my head and quietly answered, "I don't know."

Yawning and heading out the door toward his room one more time he said quietly over his shoulder, "If I live to tell about this ... nobody would believe me!"

I closed my door behind him and turned back toward the bed, removing my shirt and pants. I sat on the edge of the bed near the candle I had lit and examined the scratches my arms from the encounter downstairs. "I'll live," I whispered to myself, "although I don't know if that's so great, anyway."

I laid down on the bed and closed my eyes and exhaled deeply. In an instant I felt a body next to mine, conforming to my shape, kissing me on the neck. I rolled over facing her and we put our arms around each other and drew very close.

"There is so little time left for us," she whispered.

We held each other for another hour before a rumbling started in the house so strong it nearly shook the bed from under me. I jumped up and put on my shirt, pants, and shoes and headed for the door where Adam met me, eyes wide open. "Let's get down there and investigate!" I whispered. We rushed from the room with Karen behind us pleading, "Please! Please don't go down there! Please don't go down there! Your lives are in danger down there! Alex! Adam! Can't you hear me? Don't you understand? You're in danger down there!" I could still hear her voice fading away saying, "Alex! Adam! Don't do it! Don't go down there!"

We ran down the stairs as fast as we could, this time each using a flashlight instead of a candle, and headed straight for the noise that seemed to be coming from the library. The vibration, like an earthquake, was growing stronger as we approached the library and the ominous moaning and tightness in the air grew stronger again.

A House

We opened the library doors and the room was alive with flashing white balls of light tearing amid blobs of black and thundering voices shrieking and pounding the very walls. There was so much activity in the room it was like a haunted fun house with faces and sights and sounds made to frighten little children of things adults knew better than to fear. But now they were here and they were real and we did not feel safe. And the strongest pounding, the loudest screams of anguish, came from the end of the room where the safe was hidden!

Adam and I desperately ran for the end of the room where the safe was, despite grabbing and bumping and punching from the dark blobs streaking about the room and the deafening, screeching screams all around us. This time even I could hear their words of anguish. "Get out!" "Death!" "Kill the conspirators!" "Living leaches!" Everything was happening at once and confusing us to no end.

We finally arrived at the site of the safe and it was open and emptied! Adam and I both got close enough to flash our lights inside and, just as we came in physical contact with the safe, we were both thrown across the room, landing on the long table in the center. My face ached like I had been struck with a mighty blow from someone who, obviously, did not like my presence in the room!

More intense shouts of "Get out!" and "Kill the dogs!" and "You let him in to steal again!" screamed in our ears so intense it hurt. Adam and I scurried off the table and ran from the room.

The screaming and pushing and punching followed us from the room and down the hall and partway up the stairs where the physical contact ended and the screaming followed us no further. We ran up the stairs and immediately to the old man's room.

I banged angrily on the door. "Open up, old man! Open up! We want to have a word with you!"

The old man came to the door, his face wide with terror. "What do you want?" he screamed at the top of his fragile lungs.

Adam and I stopped and looked at each other. "Wait a minute!" Adam exclaimed. "If he'd been downstairs then why didn't we pass him along the way?"

The guide was breathing like the devil himself had visited. "Why are you trying to frighten me so? I've done nothing! I heard the screams and felt the pounding and stayed here in my room in fear of my life!"

His face turned from one of fear to one of anger. "Now get out! Leave me alone!"

Adam and I had calmed down a little. We apologized to the old man, closed his door, and returned to our rooms. The pounding and screaming from downstairs began to die away and we said nothing else as we returned to our rooms.

The pounding of the thunder outside and the flashing of the lightening stayed for a very long time. A muted rumbling and shrieking could still be heard from the library and I knew things were not going very well. I began to wonder if, in fact, I would live to see daylight again, after allowing the old man, or somebody, to rob the safe downstairs.

I wanted to believe it must have been someone else from outside our group that had the courage to enter

A House

the house during the night to rob the safe. The perfect alibi, I thought. Three of us in the house and we'd be blaming each other for the robbery. And so would the police, if they were to hear about it. Of course, I really wanted to blame the old man. After all, he'd been down there when I'd opened that very same safe earlier in the evening so, even if he'd forgotten the combination from his earlier days within the house, I stupidly refreshed his memory and allowed him to help himself.

But if he had robbed the safe, how could he have gotten past Adam and I? He would have had to come up the stairs past us at some point, I kept telling myself, so why hadn't we seen him?

Karen did not return and I wondered why. I missed her so badly I whispered for her over and over but she didn't come back. And then, at about 5:30 in the morning, with the house as quiet as death itself, I heard one shriek and muffled gurgle coming from downstairs. Strange, I thought, it would not be Karen's death reenactment. She was not supposed to have died downstairs!

I met Adam at the doorway to my room and we gingerly walked back down the long, steps again. There was still an unnerving silence in the house as though everything was right with the world. Had I not known better I would have thought this was just an old house, vacant for many years, but just an old house.

We headed for the library again, guessing that it was the center of all activity in the house. And, not to our great surprise, it was, in fact, where the activity had taken place. There, on the floor near the second safe, laid the old guide—dead.

Adam and I went to the guide's body and turned it over from its stomach to its back. A look of absolute horror was etched into the man's face and black marks were still visible around his throat. In one hand he held a large quantity of money, in the other, a small book, like a diary. Above his fallen body was the second safe, still open, money from it hanging out and scattered over the bookcases and floor, jewelry strewn across the room.

As the beam from my flashlight crossed the floor looking at the scattered money I noticed a note rubbed into the dust on the carpet as though someone had finger-painted it. It said, "Elias Johnson's debt is paid."

The room seemed to warm with a gentle breeze. The air seemed fresh, the first time the air had smelled fresh since we'd entered the house. The wind outside, although still blowing, sounded more like a mother hushing a child to sleep than a threat.

I chanced taking out the guide's wallet to look at his identification. The name on it: Elias Johnson.

Adam questioned. "But why would he continue living in the village under the same name all these years?"

"Why not?" I asked. "Remember, technically, he was never implicated in the murders. If he'd suddenly left town he might have been more suspect. But he didn't. He continued, like the rest of the family staff, never hinting that he was any less innocent than the rest of them."

Adam nodded his head. "And I guess he figured he could not spend the money because, if he did, it would attract attention toward his lifestyle and make him more suspicious."

A House

I sighed. "I wouldn't be surprised if he hadn't returned from time to time and take a little of the cash out of here just to live on."

"He may have figured that, in a small town like this, showing too much money around would be a dead giveaway so, to play it safe, he probably returned with each 'ghost hunter' and pilfered a little more money to live on. Of course, the ghosts of the house, in utter anger, would put on quite a show for the others the guide would bring with him. They would think it was just the anger of the house when, in reality, it was the anger toward the man slowly stealing the resources of the McNome family!"

I smirked a little. "I guess, tonight, he just got a little too greedy, coming back a second time like this. He probably figured we were getting too close to the answers to the crimes and he'd better take as much as he could while he had the chance."

Adam's face blanched. "But, I wonder, would he have returned upstairs and attempted to murder us in our sleep? After all, we'd come close to discovering the evidence to link him to the crimes."

I shook my head. "I can't say for sure, but, think about it— he knew all we'd really discovered was some ravings you'd made about his name. Do you think anyone would have believed just that in a court of law?" Adam shook his head. "I don't think so, either. So, I figure, he felt, as long as he could find that second diary, the one we'd mentioned to him that was supposed to have incriminated him, he'd still be safe and it would literally be our word against his."

"Of course," Adam added, "and who would believe two 'kooks' like us compared to a member of the community that has been here almost forever?"

I nodded. "So, figuring, at least, that there was a good chance the curse on the house might be lifted after this night, he took a chance and attempted one last big take to last him the rest of his days."

We looked down at his rigid body and the frozen gasp of terror on his face. "And I guess the money did last him the rest of his days. It just turned out the number was slightly less than he'd figured!" Adam mused.

We figured our job was almost done. I took the small book out of the dead man's hand with some difficulty and opened it. It was, in fact, Karen's diary. The later pages of the book did mention the thefts in the house but there was no mention of who was suspected of having committed the thefts. It was then Adam pointed out the last one or two pages appeared to have been torn out of the book. We stopped and looked at each other. Simultaneously we said, "The day of the murders."

I stood and shook my head. "Our job isn't over, Adam. We still have two more tasks to complete before we can leave this house. We must find the missing page to this book and find Karen's body and murder weapon. If we don't do it before dawn, she will still be condemned to roam these halls and now, possibly, without the rest of her family."

Chapter 9
A Troubled Dawn

I knew where we had to go. It was nearly six o'clock by then and the first hints of dawn were growing outside. I climbed the stairs to the second floor and turned to the right, away from where our rooms were, and headed into the first bedroom there toward the front of the house. Adam looked curiously at me as I walked right up to the full-length mirror in the right front corner of the room and lightly tapped its molding on the right side about chest high. The door behind it silently opened revealing the staircase behind. Adam's face lit up.

We started up the dark staircase and I kept rethinking the statement the councilwoman had made about passing the house when she was a child and seeing the light high in the right tower as she stood looking at the house. If the lights down on the first floor followed the events in the death of the parents then the light on the third floor must follow the death of Karen.

Eventually we came to the door on the third floor. It would not open. We both pushed repeatedly and it would not budge. I looked at my watch. Exactly six a.m. I heard a quiet moan come from the other side of the door and I screamed out, "Karen? Karen, is that you? Wait for us, Karen! Wait for us!"

G. Voyten

For a moment there was a strong feeling of darkness and cold and I felt very terrified. I could hear movement in the room beyond like someone tossing in their sleep and coughing. There was a dull moan coming from around and below us and it grew louder by the minute. And then we could hear pounding like hands flailing against the floor and legs beating down. My breathing became restricted and I noticed Adam grabbing at his throat and motioning like he was not breathing properly. It got darker and colder every minute, every second. The staircase, the door, the very walls of the tower, began to shake and hiss and sweat. It went on for ten minutes. Fifteen minutes. Twenty minutes. And then there was one muffled terrifying scream. And then there was absolute silence and the temperature and brightness of the stairwell returned, the vibration and moaning subsided. All again seemed normal and deathly quiet.

I tried the door again. It instantly and silently opened. This time, having flashlights, we had no difficulty making our way in the ink black room. There was more light coming in from the stairwell than there was from our flashlights so Adam thought he'd find the nearest window first and open the drapes.

As he moved away I found my way to the chair I had sat in the first time I had entered the room. There was an overpowering smell of Karen's perfume hanging in the air. I felt like I could still hear the tinkling melodious sounds of her airy voice wafting through the room, brightening things without opening a single drape. A tear ran down my face and my heart was breaking. Then, from the dark, her voice in the softest whisper tried to console me. "Do not weep for

A House

me. I am about to go on to a much better place. My family is with me and we know, within this day, you will set us all free."

Across the room from where Karen first stood I could vaguely make out the shape of her body standing in the midst of the darkness. I stood slowly and approached, tears streaming down my face. "Karen!" I paused and calmed myself down. "Can I ... hold you one last time?"

She put her arms out to me in the darkness and I went to her. We held each other so tightly it felt like no force would be able to pull us apart. I could feel the cool tears from her eyes soaking into my shoulder and I knew my tears were striking the top of her blonde head. I whispered back to her one last time, "I will love you now and forever, Karen McNome. Now and forever. I promise..."

And then Adam opened the drapes and light seeped into the room. I ignored him and he searched around the room quickly looking for what we had determined was the inevitable: Karen's body. And it did not take him long to discover it.

"I found her," he quietly whispered in the house of silence. His voice seemed muted, a million miles away and completely without emotion. I had believed he was taking it quite impersonally until I vaguely made out sobbing coming from him, very quietly.

She remained holding me tightly, facing Adam while my back remained toward him. She made it feel like she did not want me to see her in the condition her physical body actually was but, rather, to remember her always as she was there in my arms at that very moment.

She whispered in my ear, "I was the last to go. I had hidden in this room from Elias after my parents were killed but he had known this was my favorite hiding place from the time I was a child. He came up here, forced the door open, and confronted me about the missing pages to my diary. I would tell him nothing. He beat me. I would not speak. Finally, in anger, he insisted it did not matter. He knocked me to the floor and repeatedly raped me for twenty minutes, the last time strangling me as he did so. But I hid the evidence from him. I let him do whatever he wanted but knew, eventually, my strength would be his undoing."

Adam had been examining the remains of Karen's body, still exactly in the position it had been at the time of her death. The dress the body wore was the same dress she wore while with me. Around her neck was one of her own scarves taken from a chest of drawers directly above her head. One hand, Adam noticed, was underneath her body.

Gently, he pulled it from behind her. Two pages of a diary were still in her hand.

He removed the pages from her grip and took them to the window. They were dated the day of her death. Reading aloud, he said, "'My parents are dead. Money has been stolen. I know the assailant is coming up the stairs for me even as I write this. Please, God, protect me from Elias Johnson or forever damn his soul with the evils he has made us suffer.'" He looked up from the paper. "And that was all she wrote."

I could feel Karen fading from my grip. Her voice was fading away as she disappeared into the only remaining darkness of the room as sunlight began

A House

streaming in through the open curtains. "We are all free now, Alex, Adam. We cannot begin to thank you enough for what you have endured and what you have done for us. Please remember what my father told you, Alex, and take the evidence to the law firm my father mentioned. The story is not over, Alex Jones, and you have not seen the last of me yet in your earthly life. Just remember I love you and watch for me in every look in every girl you meet. I'll always love you... always love you ... always love you..."

And she was gone. The house was as silent as the tomb it actually was but, somehow, the air had still a lingering trace of Karen's sweet perfume in it. The rising sun had directed a golden beam of light directly upon Karen's ancient remains before us and, somehow, the appearance of her body did not seem as shocking as before. Karen was at rest and the sun was finally warming her troubled life, preparing her for the better existence ahead.

Adam turned to me and said, "Why did she call you 'Alex Jones'? Your last name isn't 'Jones': it's Williams!"

I just shook my tired head.

"And, just as curious, what did she mean by 'watch for me in every look in every girl you meet'?"

I just looked at him and calmly said, "I don't know. But Williams was the name of the family that adopted me, not my real name. I never knew what my real name was."

"But how could people who died before your real parents were even born know the history of your life? How could they know what name you really have?"

I shook my head and looked down at Karen's body again. "I just don't know, Adam, I just don't know."

The sun was up and it was a bright and beautiful morning. I stood a long while over Karen's body and cried at the end that had come to such a kind, beautiful woman. "I pity the others, as well, Adam, but I pity Karen the most. She had not much of a life in the few years she had been upon this earth and then to have been treated so terribly in the final minutes of her existence…"

After awhile we went back down the staircase to the second floor and came out through the mirror again. Adam thought of a question. "How did the guide get down to the library the first time to rob the safe without us seeing any trace of him?"

We headed toward our bedrooms but stopped at the guide's first. I went to open the door but it was locked from the inside. Strange, we thought, the guide was downstairs, dead, and yet his room was still bolted from the inside!

"Yes, and so were the doors on either end of the hall!" I laughed. We went straight downstairs and to the large living room on the same side of the house as our bedrooms. It seemed reasonable to assume that a door must exist in the front room similar to the one that existed in the den across the hall.

We looked at the room and soon observed the "odd wall" similar to the one in the other room across the hall. On it was a picture but, rather than just being hung from a nail or screw and wire, it was securely screwed to the wall on all four corners. We looked down at the dust in the carpet. "Notice the footprints

A House

coming from and going to this wall," I commented. "There must be a hidden door here somewhere."

We tapped and felt around the wall and, finally, stumbled onto the spring loaded single board that silently opened the hidden door. The seams where the door started and the wall ended were hidden well by the picture frame.

We climbed the stairway up to the second floor and pressed the panel there that opened the door going into the room the guide had occupied. Adam whispered, "No wonder the guide chose his room first. He had an ulterior motive!"

"But we should check out how he got around down on the first floor before we do anything else," I added.

We returned to the first floor for further investigation. We followed the footprints in the dust to see exactly where they led. They led out of the room toward the back of the house to the large formal dining room and then turned toward the center of the house, across the back hallway, and into the rear entrance to the library.

"So this was how Elias got to the safe and back to his room without us seeing him," Adam remarked.

We retraced our steps and returned to the guide's room. We examined it again and discovered ... nothing! Somehow, between the times Adam and I had been with the man, he must have taken what he had stolen from the safe and hidden it somewhere in the house!

I looked at Adam, the confusion written plainly on my face. "But where would he have had time to take it?"

Adam's face brightened. "Where else?"

I agreed. And we took the hidden staircase up to the third floor again, this time in a room on the opposite side from the one in which Karen's body lay. We opened the door that made no sound and were amazed at what we'd discovered. Money. Jewelry. Bonds. Stocks. Clothing. Books. Tools. And things of lesser quality— pornographic pictures, weapons, clothes bloodied long ago, axes with blood stains on the blades, letters of blackmail to a number of victims and photographs of couples in rather compromising positions. Adam looked around shaking his head. "This was not a nice man," he assured me.

Looking around I added, "I would guess this to be the room he occupied while employed here. It appears this collection was many years in the making."

Everything had been covered with thick layers of dust except one rather large box that was perfectly clean. We surmised this box was probably the one used to store the items taken from the safe during the night and brought up to the room. We opened it in such a way we kept our fingerprints from the surfaces and discovered many thousands of dollars, gold coins, rings, necklaces, and bonds from companies we weren't sure still existed. I looked at Adam and said, "He wasn't greedy or anything, was he?"

Adam laughed. "I'm surprised he didn't try prying the safe itself from the wall!"

I thought for a moment. "You know, Adam, I still can't understand why he did it! We had all experienced some pretty horrifying things during the night and yet he still had the courage to sneak down there and rob the safes!"

A House

"Unless he thought things would only happen when you and I were with him! Think about it! All the previous experiences where we encountered strange things were when we were all together. Even when he robbed the first safe he was not battered around by the ghosts in the library—WE were! And Mr. McNome had told you he planned on letting the murderer get involved by subliminally suggesting it to him in the first place! And I'm sure, after his first complete success and our utter failure, he thought it was we that had caused the ghosts to rise up, not himself!"

I nodded my head in agreement. "Yes, I think you're right. He may have thought we attracted the ghosts rather than himself. So he probably figured he was safe from further attacks as long as he was by himself! Or else, like I'd said earlier, he'd planned these things out over the years to know just how to 'fool' the ghosts of the house and get away with some of the money to support himself."

I changed the subject. "But now we've got to get our gear together and leave here and bring the law back to investigate his death downstairs."

We headed for the staircase again. Adam added, "I just hope they don't decide to blame us for the old guy's death. After all, he was strangled and you don't need a murder weapon to pin that crime on anybody."

We exited through the guide's room and unbolted the door. We each went to the rooms we'd stayed in for the night to gather up the supplies we'd used there and I could hear Adam babbling on about something or other, mostly trivial nonsense. But, in the back of my mind, something still seemed incomplete, missing.

I plopped myself down on the bed, the bed that didn't have much use for sleeping during the night. My mind began to drift a million miles away, back to thoughts of Karen and how wonderful my time with her had been. I was daydreaming, looking down toward the floor and the patterns in the dust and the carpet, when I noticed a small, shiny object beneath a small three legged table standing next to the bedroom door. I thought it odd being there. Why had I not noticed it the day before when it had still been light outside? Or was it necessary for it to be morning light? Or did Karen leave me a gift?

Adam was still talking about something across the hall, in another world, when I dropped to my knees to retrieve whatever was beneath that table. And, to my utter amazement, it was a small brass key, the kind used to lock up small "keepsake" style wooden boxes—like the kind sitting next to the photograph of Karen on the vanity!

I thought it had to just be a coincidence. Then I thought, so what? What could it possibly be that could be worth the effort to walk all the way over there, a whole ten feet, and see if it did, in fact, fit into that little chest? And, even if it did, what difference would it make?

But it did. I gathered some lame strength and forced myself back to my feet and all the way over there to the vanity and the little wooden box sitting atop it.

Just as I put the key in the lock Adam came bouncing into the room, still talking about something that was probably very important in his own mind,

A House

when he saw what I was doing and stopped himself in mid sentence and said calmly, "What are you doing?"

I said, "Oh, nothing. Playing with the past, I guess." And I attempted to turn the key.

The lock would not move at first. I thought I'd chosen poorly and the key and lock actually did not go together. But then Adam thought otherwise and came over to give it a try.

When he touched the key he moved back a bit and said, "There's something special about this little key." He paused as he jiggled the key within the lock and we finally heard it creaking unlocked. "This key's energy tells me it is important but is only a small player in a bigger plan."

We opened the lid to the little box and, surprisingly, there was another key! This key was a little bigger and it there was a note in the bottom of the box that just said, "Spare."

Adam picked up the second key. "This key's energy tells me it is a little more important than the first, but is still not as important as what it is protecting."

I held the key in my hand and tapped it against my lips repeating over and over, "'Spare'. 'Spare' … spare what?"

Adam held the key in his hands. "I feel Karen's energy on this key, but I feel much more of Mr. McNome's presence associated with it." He rubbed it a few more seconds and looked up. "Why do I keep getting a picture of a large bedroom? Like…"

I smiled at Adam and we hurried out of Karen's bedroom, down the hall to the opposite end of the house, to the master bedroom of Karen's parents. Up until that time I had not been in that room and Adam admitted he and the guide only searched the obvious: furniture, the bed, the closets. But I was coming to feel this room hid a safety deposit box that the key in my hand went to.

I thought about the notebook Brian McNome had given me but I thought I'd try my luck at impressions first. Adam and I began to systematically check out the room for a small safe and, in a matter of seconds, I stumbled onto it.

The safe was, again, behind a painting. Gee, I thought couldn't these people be more original with their locations? But I went ahead and put the key in the lock and gave it a turn. Surprisingly, it turned easily and the safe door swung open.

The contents of the safe were a little disappointing. Some family papers, a few dollars, some jewelry, and another key! And this key had stamped on it "B. Vault".

Adam's eyes grew as large as saucers. "Vault? Vault?" he kept repeating. "All the little safes around here and they also have a vault?"

"Let's give this a little thought, Adam. A vault has to be a fairly good size, right?"

"Right," he agreed.

"And what do you think that 'B' stands for?"

"Backup? Bedroom? Backyard?"

I thought for a minute. "What about basement?"

So we took a trip back to the basement, a place that held fond and not so fond memories for me but, for the most part, Adam had not experienced. We both had flashlights with us and we systematically began looking at each of the rooms again, The playroom. The

A House

canning room. The furnace room. Storage rooms. Tool rooms. Work shops. The laundry room. And finally, although not to my liking, the room that also had the entrance to the tunnel.

The room that also had the tunnel door was the largest room in the basement, rivaling even the furnace room. There was furniture and other entertainment items present and many doors, most which actually went nowhere. It was as though the designers were trying to create an illusion that this room was somewhere else, like a train station or other public transit point. One of those doors actually led to the tunnel as I'd discovered the previous day. One other, we eventually discovered, actually hid the vault. But the key I had found in the master bedroom was not to the vault itself but, rather, to the door hiding the vault!

With the wooden door unlocked and opened, the steel door to the vault stood before us. Adam and I grinned from ear to ear at each other and each took a deep breath and exhaled. But, since neither of us were safe crackers, I relied on the little handbook Mr. McNome had given me to reveal the combination.

We nervously entered the combination, Adam holding the flashlight somewhat steady for me while I read the combination from the encrypted notebook and entered the numbers. And, after entering the final digit, I nervously turned the handle and heard a snap inside the safe door.

With both excitement and fear we jointly pulled the heavy door open. It cracked and whined but didn't give much resistance once it was in motion. I was very apprehensive about allowing light to enter the safe but did so just the same.

It was incredible! The vault was the size of a room with many shelves holding items from precious gold coins, unset jewels, historic artifacts dating from early Egyptian to the Renaissance, paintings, Spanish gold treasure. It was like a miniature museum held inside one moderate sized room!

We stood in awe; mouths wide open, not really knowing what to say. I tried to speak. "It's like ... finding King Tut's tomb!"

Adam's face changed from one in splendid shock to one in splendid pleasure! A grin spread from ear to ear and he started laughing, soft at first, and then louder and louder. I started laughing when he started laughing and, in no time, our laughter echoed throughout the basement!

Adam stopped to try to catch his breath. "Alex, I don't know what to say! I never expected to find anything like this in a zillion, billion years!"

I'd stopped laughing, wiping the tears from my tired eyes. "We'd better close up shop on this thing before we get it in our head to keep it a secret and walk off with something!"

Still smiling, Adam added, "And you can bet Mr. McNome would get us if we tried something like that!"

"You bet! So make sure nothing sticks to your hands or pockets!" I chuckled back.

And nothing did. We closed up the vault, closed up the wooden door, relocked everything, put furniture back in front of the doorway, and walked back up to the bedrooms.

We gathered up all our gear from the rooms and the kitchen and slowly trekked out to the car and slammed everything back into the trunk. We started the

A House

car and headed off the dead end street and drove back to the police station less than a mile away.

Chapter 10
Back To Civilization

*O*n our short trip Adam and I wanted, somehow, to confirm to each other that what we had just been through in the last twenty-four hours had, indeed, happened. As we discussed things, there was almost an embarrassment in our voices as though we wanted to apologize to each other for needing to explain ourselves better.

Adam had to remark about what had happened to me in such a short time. "I've got to admit, Alex, you surprised me on this adventure!"

I smiled. "What do you mean, Adam?"

He grinned. "Well, for one thing, you had more psychic experiences in this one trip than in all our other trips combined! Besides, in just this trip, you confirmed the existence of spiritual manifestations in such a way anyone experiencing them would not have to be convinced such things exist!"

I laughed. "I guess you could say that! After all, it's not very often people are beaten up by things that don't exist!"

"And what about Karen?" He exhaled deeply, the smile on his face leaving. "I mean, was that something or what? I just absolutely could not believe her!"

"What do you mean?"

He shook his head. "It wasn't enough that she was the first ghost we'd ever seen. It wasn't enough that the way she appeared to us was as a whole, solid person, not like the images we'd observed down in the library, but she had to be beautiful and she had to be in love with a guy that has never had a pretty girl give him the time of day before in his life!"

I nodded my head. "Yeah. So what?"

Under his breath I could just make out something that sounded like one of the words it contained was "jealous."

"Jealous? Did I hear the great lady killer say he was jealous?" I laughed out loud.

"Well, yes, I was jealous." And he looked at me and smiled. "But it was so great seeing you with a beautiful girl that wasn't out to use you for something!"

I smiled. "Thanks, Adam. I felt it was nice to have a woman love me once in my life, too. It was just a shame it didn't last for more than one day!"

We prepared to pull up to the police station and pick up the chief of police. We parked the car and slowly walked into the station, dragging our tired bones up to the dispatcher.

We met the chief there and told him the outcome of our night in the house. He was interested in checking things out himself but wanted the other officials of the township present, as well, since Adam and I were requested to solve the mystery by a township committee, not by one individual.

He notified the law firm, the coroner, and the mayor's office and all of us, including most of the members of the town council, headed back to the mansion.

It had been no more than an hour from the time we'd left until we'd arrived back at the house and we headed straight for the library to show them the body of the guide who, by the way, all the townspeople were familiar with but none seemed to really know his name. By the time we'd entered the library it was bright daylight and golden beams of sunshine filtered through the trees and filled the room.

But none would fall on the body of the guide. Somehow, amid all the bright sunlight in the rest of the room, the guide's body was still in shadow behind the column of a wall frame.

The chief moved to the body to examine it with the help of the coroner. But, turning the body over to look at the face the coroner gasped. "Why, this body has been dead for years!

Adam and I reacted immediately preparing to argue the point that, in fact, the man had been dead less than two hours. We were prepared to argue until we looked down at the face of the guide that was dried and parched like an Egyptian mummy, the features nearly unrecognizable but the stare of terror still carved in the bleached skin. However the diary was still held in his hand!

Adam looked at me. "I thought we'd removed that book and examined the pages!" he whispered.

I whispered back, "We had. But something unexplainable is going on here!"

The coroner and the chief asked to see the evidence of Karen's body. We told them we'd have to go upstairs for that. And, when Adam led the way out of the room I put the diary in my pocket. Whispering to

A House

myself I said, "That'll be the last time this book will move on its own!"

All of us climbed the central stairway to the second floor and, one by one, made our way up through the tower staircase to the third floor. The noise was rather sizable with the number of people involved all walking up those stairs at the same time. I thought the sight would have been comical if not for the reason we were all there. And in very little time the entire group had crowded into Karen's little hidden room. There, exactly as we'd originally found the body, Karen's remains laid.

The number of people there formed a sizable crowd that arched around Karen and I could not bear to be that close to her body again. I found myself compelled to withdraw to the corner of the room near the tower staircase where Karen had appeared and disappeared in the room. And, as the members of the investigation party were mumbling and remarking about what they were observing, I felt gentle hands on the back of my arms, as I had the first time I'd met Karen, and felt a face draw tantalizingly close to the back of my head so I could feel breath against the back of my neck, as I had with Karen, and the gentle fragrance of Karen's perfume wafting past my nose. But before I could make a movement or a comment a gentle, familiar voice whispered in my ear, the breath blowing the hairs on my neck, "I thought I'd never find you!"

I dashed to turn around, my face beaming with delight! I reached to embrace Karen again and tell her just how much I loved and missed her!

But it was not Karen! IT WAS NOT <u>KAREN</u>!

Shock ran through my body like a bolt of lightening and my face blanked. I didn't know what to say! There stood a remarkably beautiful red haired woman with deep red lips, pale pink skin, and piercing green eyes staring deep into my eyes with a knowing look that told me we had known each other for a very, very long time. A slight smile was on her lips and her look told me she held feelings for me that went as deep as emotions could bear.

I tried to piece myself back together and stop looking like a complete idiot. My heart was racing a million miles an hour and I felt weak like I was going to pass out. My mouth dried and my hands moistened as my forehead perspired and I frantically searched for words. Breathlessly, I replied, "Oh! I thought you were someone else!"

Still looking deep into my eyes, never removing her stare, she answered, "I am someone else!" A sly smile now emerged and I fought to understand if she meant what I thought she meant or if she was just trying to be witty.

I began to calm down, although only slightly. "I'm sorry! You reminded me of someone ... someone I know very, very well and care for very much that used to live around here ..."

Her eyes softened from an intense, knowing stare to one of affection. Still in a whisper she replied, "Well, I live around here and I think I knew that person very well." A very intense, piercing look came to her eyes again. "*Very* well." Still staring, her face coming so close our noses nearly touched. She whispered even softer, "I could almost say ... *intimately*."

A House

I was nearly loosing it! How could that happen? How could some woman, out of the blue, come up to me and do that to me? But I didn't want to read more into the conversation than what had really been said. After all, I was an investigator and knew facts had to be compiled and analyzed before drawing conclusions. So I tried to make the assumption this woman was just toying with me.

She stopped making the intense looks at me and took on a more casual, businesslike look. "But we haven't been introduced yet. My name is Kristen. Kristen Smith. I'm one of the legal partners in the firm that manages this estate."

I sighed a breath of relief! "Oh! Hi! And my name is …"

"… Alex Jones," she interrupted.

Another shock coursed through my body! That was the name Karen had called me, not the name I had given people! I attempted to correct her. "No, Alex Williams."

She laughed a little. "Actually, your name is Alex Jones. My firm has researched you and your family for quite some time and I'm sure you will find we probably know more about you than you know about yourself."

Somehow I didn't think the day was going to get any better. I remembered Karen using that exact same phrase, about knowing more about me than I knew about myself, and it didn't make me feel any too confident in myself. I felt I might as well try to make the best of it. I shook the woman's extended hand and replied, "It's nice to meet you."

She actually grinned from ear to ear. "After you spend some time in our offices I think you'll even be more glad!"

I had no idea of what she was talking about but it didn't matter, since the crowd around Karen's body was heading toward us. The coroner and the chief were discussing what they'd found. "Yes, Mr. Williams, it seems obvious the handyman, Elias Johnson, must have had something to do with this woman's death. We found two pages to her diary naming him as the murderer." He handed me the pages. I took them and reinserted them into the original book that I'd removed from my pocket. The pages in their original place, I put the book safely away again in my coat pocket.

Adam volunteered, "We can show you where Elias Johnson stored the items he had stolen. And various other items, some of which are not so nice."

Before leaving the room the chief got on a walkie talkie and called his office. "You'd better send for the county forensics team, John. Have them meet us over at the old McNome place. There's a body on the third floor and one on the first to be removed. Signal when you're ready and I'll direct you to their locations."

Adam and I spent much of the morning showing the group the things we'd discovered through the previous day and night. We opened the door out of Karen's secret room and, for the first time for any of us, saw the remainder of the third floor. The ultimate intent, of course, was to go directly down the hall to Elias Johnson's room and show the collection of things there. Adam, anxious to lead the investigation, rapidly made his way down to the room and took the party members inside, talking loudly and proudly the entire

A House

time. Not being someone particularly comfortable in public, I stayed toward the back of the group and let them get away from me. Having Adam volunteer to do all the talking was perfect with me.

While Adam was busy explaining how Elias had been using the other investigations as a way of resupplying himself with living expenses and showing the murder weapons and some of the stolen items, I strayed into the other rooms. I casually wandered from room to room, trying to figure out whom the rooms might belong to. It appeared the hired help occupied much of the third floor because there was evidence of domestic supplies in many of the rooms, things like white aprons and a few black and white uniforms. It appeared the staff did not take much of the domestic reminders with them when they left for the last time.

I constantly had the feeling I was being watched and, finally, moving from one common entertainment center where the staff could gather and relax, I turned around rather suddenly and found the lady lawyer staring at me from the doorway! But, when I saw her, she immediately lost all confidence and acted like she didn't know what excuse to use to explain her presence. But I didn't ask for one. Instead, I invited her to accompany me through the rooms.

We slowly made our way from room to room, never really doing much other than looking, not even touching things. I occasionally sneaked a look at her and, from the corner of my eye, noticed her doing the same to me. Throughout the entire time we were always very close, nearly touching in everything we did. It was almost like having a child with me that mimicked everything I did. If I'd lift up a framed photograph and put it down, she would come up after me and do the same thing. If I looked outside at the view from the room, she would wait until I was finished and do the same again.

Finally, wondering what she was trying to do and why she was following me around so, I started a conversation with her. I really didn't know what to say, being rather shy around women and having been caught so off guard by that one in particular, but I tried, nonetheless. I thought I'd attempt to explain why I was so interested in every little thing about the old home. "I'm trying so hard to experience the essence of this house. I'm trying to learn the lifestyle that must have existed here in its prime."

She looked at me with a surprised but pleased look on her pretty face. Smiling, she answered, "That's good. It's good to try to understand there was more to this place than just the bad things people remember."

I sighed as I lifted a photograph of a young man and woman close to each other, beaming from ear to ear. "I'd like to think of this place more like the happy event that must have taken place during this photograph rather than the tragedy that occurred later."

Kristen looked down at the photograph. "Yes, this photo of Ivis and Frank was taken out in back behind the arbor on a beautiful summer's day about two months before she quit and got married."

"I sure hope they lived happily ever after."

She smiled. "Yes, they moved to Ohio and never knew of the events that happened here."

We turned back into the room and slowly walked toward the door leading to the central hallway. I asked, "How large was the staff here?"

A House

"The staff was never larger than seven, including the handyman who also doubled as a chauffeur."

"And do you think the staff cared for the McNome family? Or do you think they tolerated them because they were employed by them?"

"Oh, the staff deeply cared for the McNome family. It was said the women staff members, four of the seven employees in the household, actually went into deep mourning after the discovery of the McNome deaths."

I left the room, Kristen at my side bumping off my arm, shaking my head saying, "What a shame, what a shame …"

We caught up to the rest of the group just as they were finishing looking at Elias' room and were heading down the circular staircase that would lead to the room he had occupied during our stay. From there we headed into the room I had stayed in and showed the group the toolbox containing the money and the knife used to kill Mrs. McNome. The chief immediately took control of the toolbox before anyone had a chance to touch any of the contents, including the knife.

We continued down through the circular stairway to the first floor and we showed the group how Elias had exited into the front sitting room and gone through the back of the house to the library to rob the safe without us seeing him do it. And, after all that, the chief was anxious to see the tunnel that Adam had mentioned repeatedly throughout the morning, especially when we presented the toolbox.

But, when it came to the tunnel, I became a little nervous. I had not experienced what I would call a good time in the tunnel and, as much as I'd hoped things there were right with the world, I still had bad feelings about it. Somehow, I felt something was still wrong there, something was still evil there, something was destined to give me another bad, bad time there. And, for some strange reason, most people don't head back into things that have hurt them once. What's that expression about "once bitten, twice shy"?

Throughout the morning and the tour and the explanations the woman I'd met that morning stayed ever beside me so close her body frequently bounced off mine as we walked. Even during my conversation with the council members when I'd sneak a glance at her I'd notice her staring up at me, very much like Karen had done when she'd said she wanted to learn my face so as not to ever forget me. But it was not until we all went to the basement I knew she was the woman Karen had told me to watch for.

We all entered the basement, two at a time going down the stairs, Kristen and I first. I'd explained where the coal bin was and the way to the tunnel and the group wandered off leaving Kristen and I relatively alone. Adam, again, made things easier for me by forcing himself to the front, as it were, even though the only experience he'd had with the basement was when we'd gone off on our treasure hunt earlier in the day. But as before, I wasn't too anxious to be with the group so I allowed Adam to dominate the tour while I brought up the rear, so to speak. Without even thinking I went by myself to the toy room where I had spent one of my most memorable moments with Karen and I immediately returned to the table where her favorite doll was and picked it up and, again, cleaned the

A House

humidity and grime from its glass face. I smiled down at it and sighed a heavy sigh thinking strongly and fondly of Karen and what could be no more.

And then, quietly, gently, from behind me, a familiar voice that sounded like a wind chime whispered to me, "That was my favorite doll when I was a child."

I spun around and saw the backlit outline of a woman standing in the doorway, just where I'd found Karen the previous night. In a loud whisper I answered, "Karen? Is that you?"

The dark image approached slowly, head bent low, looking down at the doll. Again, in a voice barely audible, she said, "I told you I would find a way to come back to you if I could. Now hold me!"

I wrapped my arms around her and our bodies molded together like one, her face nestling again to my neck, a kiss placed there. But this time her body felt warm—her tears warm. Even her kiss felt warm.

I drew us apart and looked down at the woman I'd been holding. In horror I loudly whispered, <u>"You're not Karen!"</u>

The woman looked up at me, tears streaming from her green eyes. Still whispering, she replied, "Yes, I am. On the inside!"

Tears filled my eyes. I was so frustrated I didn't know what to say or do. I began to tremble. "But how can you be Karen? Karen's gone. She's dead!"

Sobbing, she answered, "She's here. We're both here!"

I shook my head. "I don't understand!"

Kristen pulled herself close to me again, her lips near my ear. "I know everything about Karen. I know

G. Voyten

everything about you. Just as Karen visited you in your dreams, so she did with me. But now she is a part of me for the rest of my life! When I came to understand just how much she loved you, I agreed to become one with her! I am the girl she told you to watch for!"

I pulled her tighter to me. "But how could YOU care for me? You don't even know me!"

She sniffed her nose and tried to laugh. "I have known you for the last two years! I have dreamed of you, through Karen, for the last two years! I knew what you looked like long before I saw you standing there today. I have seen you more than any other man in my life, outside of my family! I can even tell you everything you experienced with Karen last night!"

That thought embarrassed me. Timidly I asked, "Everything?"

She giggled. "<u>Every</u>thing!"

Still unsure I whispered, 'Even the part where ..."

"... She took off her clothes and ..."

I interrupted immediately, "I believe you—that's enough!"

She giggled again and pulled her body tight to mine, just as Karen had done. The hug was so intimate I closed my eyes, just as though we'd kissed. I whispered, not expecting an answer, "I can't believe this is happening to me!"

Kristen answered back, "I can't believe it's finally happening to me, either!"

"What do you mean, 'finally'?" I asked.

She hugged harder. "We've planned this for at least the last six months! As soon as Karen convinced me where to look for you and I'd discovered where you

A House

lived and how to get in touch with you, we planned this happening!"

"But I still don't understand! I'd never met Karen and yet, somehow, she convinced me she loved me and, in a short period of time, I came to love her as well. That alone was incredible to try to believe since, in all my life, no woman ever loved me like Karen had in just those few hours. It is easy to love someone when no one has ever loved you and, suddenly, someone does and does so strongly. So I came to believe she loved me. But <u>you</u>—why would you care for me? You've never met me before!"

She sighed against my chest. "Oh, but I <u>have</u>! I have seen you in my dreams for a long time. Karen and I shared you in my dreams. As I came to understand what Karen loved in you, so did I. So, you see, not only did I share thoughts with her I shared her feelings and came to the same conclusion about you! Being able to see a man's heart before meeting him and having to put up with that entire superficial courtship facade helps a lot. I've grown to love your heart, not your image!"

I pulled away from her just enough to look down into those green eyes and run my fingers through that shock of red hair. "I think I love both of you!" I whispered. And I kissed her very softly for a long time.

She whispered back, "And we both love you."

I held her for a few moments before I heard Adam calling for me. It was obvious the group was not having much luck finding additional clues in the basement and Adam wanted me to help. But, before he got to me, I hastily whispered, "But how are we going to explain all this to this crowd out there?"

Kristen smiled a warm, comfortable smile. "Let's just act as acquaintances today and I'll make up for it later."

"Agreed," I said as we headed out of the room. I hugged her and wrapped my arm briefly around her waist and she hugged me with one arm. "But we've got an awful lot of talking to do later!"

She giggled again and dried her eyes. "More than you can imagine!"

Adam was in the long hallway looking for me and balked when he saw me walking with Kristen. Staring terribly obviously at her but speaking to me he said, "Alex ... they're looking for you." An unnatural pause later he added, this time speaking to Kristen, "Excuse me, but ... do we know each other? Somehow you look very familiar to me."

Kristen blossomed into a broad grin but said nothing. I instructed Adam, "Touch her face a second, Adam."

He followed my instructions and instantly jumped back against the wall in amazement. <u>"Karen!"</u>

Shock covered Kristen's face! She looked at me like death itself had touched her. "Alex! How did he know?"

Now I was grinning! I laughed, "Adam is my psychic friend! And now I'm sure you understand that he is not faking!"

Adam looked at me. "But Alex ... <u>how</u>?"

Smiling, I answered, "Adam, this is Kristen. Kristen Smith of Smith and Edwards, remember? It seems Kristen and Karen have been friends for quite some time! And, a while ago, they made a deal that, when the time came for Karen to depart, she would

A House

merge personalities with Kristen, if she could, and the two would continue living as one."

His face, still in shock, staring at Kristen, continued, "Does that mean that ... Kristen cares for you already?"

Kristen wrapped both arms around my right upper arm and smiled back at Adam. "Yes, I have known Alex for a long time and I care for him very much," she said softly.

Adam leaned up against the hall wall and wiped his perspiring forehead. "I can't believe this! All these years I've known you and you've never had any luck with women and now, all of a sudden, two of the most beautiful women I have ever seen in all my life are hanging all over you!"

I laughed quietly. "Maybe I should take up religion?"

He chuckled. "It's too late, pal. You probably could start your own religion!"

Chapter 11
The Town and the Tunnel

We headed toward the group and found them waiting for us at the entrance to the tunnel, all faces looking at us as we approached. Adam and I both had flashlights as did various members of the group and I could tell some members were a little uneasy about entering the utter blackness of the tunnel.

I did not hesitate starting into the tunnel and quietly commented, "Ladies and gentlemen, I hope things go better this time for us all than they went for me yesterday afternoon when I tried this the first time."

The mayor asked, "What exactly happened?"

I hesitated, not wanting to sound like some kind of nut case. "Let's just say it was an intriguing experience with a few surprises along the way. And the rats and snakes were not the most challenging of the encounters."

The lady council member replied, "There were things worse than rats and snakes to face?"

I laughed a fake laugh. "Ma'am, a room full of rats somehow would seem like a day in the park compared to what we may be preparing to encounter up ahead." I paused and my face grew steely serious. "There is great evil in this place." I paused. My voice lowered in tone and volume. "I just hope the evil has gone or, at least, diminished, since last night."

A House

We slowly, very slowly began walking down the black tunnel, the quantity of lights still bright enough to keep spirits high but the ever present blackness always ahead of us keeping everyone apprehensive. The combined sounds of our steps sounded like a thousand walkers when echoed from an infinitely long chamber ahead and behind us. In the distance I could vaguely hear a low moaning noise, just like that heard during the various dark spiritual encounters Adam and I had experienced at the worst of the night. If it had been just something in my head, I thought, I would not be able to hear it echoing from the walls as well, as, in fact, I could.

The mumbling in the group diminished as the moaning became louder. The voices of the group members changed from those of people merely making conversation to those near panic.

I looked at Adam. Whispering, I said, "I don't have a real good feeling about this, bucko. Somehow I don't think all the evil of the house has left!"

Adam's head was nodding furiously. Hoarsely whispering he replied, "I didn't know what you went through down here yesterday but, if this is any indication, I don't think it amounted to what I'd call a good time."

We came to the remains of the vagrant still in the exact position I'd seen it the previous day. However, there were the remains of blackness around it that made me feel his soul may not have gone on to bigger and better places or something else was attempting to reanimate his body. By that time we were not walking very fast and the tunnel's temperature was dropping. As the middle of the group walked past the body on the floor I could hear the bones chattering. The low moaning sound was growing louder and the blackness seemed to grow closer.

The air grew stale and close. The humidity intensified, although it was nearly condensing on the walls as it was. In addition to the low moaning sound I could hear hissing from the walls, the floor, the ceiling. It was as though every surface was moving. I heard one member of the party behind me wheezing for breath. It was the female council member. When I looked at her she was already clutching her chest and had a pained look on her face as though she could not get her breath. I thought I'd better warn her now before things got closer to their worst. My voice, when I tried to speak, was weak and dry and tight as though I were suffering from a respiratory illness. "Ma'am, if you're experiencing serious problems now you and some of the others might strongly consider going back to the house where it's safer."

The lady wheezed back to me, her voice so strained it was nearly a whisper. "What do you mean? What's happening?"

Adam answered, choking and wheezing with every breath. "Evil, Ma'am. Pure evil. Somehow, contrary to what we'd believed would take place, much of the evil that had existed in this house and, especially, in this tunnel, never left when the curse was lifted from the McNome family."

I continued, my eyes now beginning to burn, my voice still weak and strained. "We had thought the evil would be transformed into Elias Johnson at the time of his death but, possibly because his body is still upstairs

A House

and has not been sanctified, it appears much of it remains with us down here."

The chief got back on his radio. The static was strong, not because of the happenings in the tunnel but because of the tunnel itself—radios do not work well below ground. Through the static, though, he could still contact his office. In a voice weak and labored he called, "Send the priest and an ambulance squad to the McNome mansion and have him bless the body of the old man located in the library and remove the body from the house. And make it as fast as you can!"

The chief motioned for us to continue so we did. The moaning grew even louder and the darkness began closing in. I looked over at Adam to see how well he was doing and saw a troubled look on his face. I whispered, "Adam, are you gonna be ok?"

He gasped and wheezed and held his chest, pain was written all over his face. "Yeah. I think so. But it would be better to have that guy removed from upstairs if we could."

The beams from the flashlights were not extending more than a few feet. The density of the air and the foul stench of death hung on our every breath. The moaning was growing so loud we would have to raise our voices to be heard above it. The temperature was probably near 40 degrees and all of us were breathing shallow, rapid, frantic breaths. The floor began to shake and the sound of the shaking combined with the moaning and the hissing. The last thirty feet had taken us fifteen minutes to walk and our every step was labored, as though being physically held back by some incredibly powerful force.

And then, abruptly, it all stopped as if by a miracle! Instantly the chief's radio crackled and a voice came on which we could all hear saying, "Ok, chief, Father Brennan has blessed the body we found in the library and the ambulance team has carefully removed it and is taking it to the coroner's office." There was a pause in the communications but we could tell the man was still holding down the transmit button of his radio. He added, "What on earth happened to this guy, anyway?"

The chief, clearing his voice, stated, "It'll all be explained later. But thanks for getting him out of here. I'm out for now." Adam, still recovering from the ordeal, spoke back to the chief in a reduced volume. "I'd suggest the priest place a crucifix directly on the chest of the body and make sure it remains there, even after the body is buried."

The chief must have still been holding down the transmit button and then, realizing it, released it. The radio crackled. "Understood. Will do," a voice replied.

The air, although not sweet, was not dense and did not smell as foul as before. The darkness was a more normal darkness, although still black ahead and behind beyond the reach of the flashlights we carried, and the temperature, although cool, was not near freezing.

In a few moments we were at the entrance to the side room where the implements of destruction were stored along with those of gardening. All entering the room moved their lights around, looking for signs of what the room contained and what secrets it might yet reveal. And there, in the opposite corner from the one in which I'd found the toolbox, hidden beneath a snow shovel, were the heads of Brian and Sarah McNome!

A House

It was then I'd noticed Kristen hanging tightly to my arm, nearly cutting off its circulation! It reminded me of the previous day with Karen in the same situation. I looked down at Kristen and a pained expression was still etched on her face. I patted her hands with my own. She muttered, "Those poor people!"

"Yes. But, hopefully, their suffering is finally over."

She looked up at me, still troubled with the scene, and replied, "Well, maybe it's not yet completely over, but it is almost over."

Additional evidence was discovered. The saws used to saw apart the bodies, still covered with blood, still showing the bloody fingerprints of Elias Johnson on the saw handle. And then I'd noticed the bloodstains all over the floor and looked directly above them.

Adam's look followed mine and he commented before I could, "I can see ropes hanging from that drainage pipe up there at the ceiling! I think the bodies were hung upside down by their feet like slaughtered pigs to drain them of their blood!"

Kristen became very impatient. "Please, Alex, let's get out of here! I don't like this place. I'm frightened. And it hurts me to just look at these things."

I squeezed her hands. "I understand," I whispered.

I moved over to Adam who was busy, like the rest, searching for evidence. In a reduced volume voice I told him, "I'm taking Kristen away from here for a while, Adam. Go ahead and stay with the others and help them investigate. We'll be close by if you need us. And be careful. Try not to touch things. It could be painful for you."

He looked at me, then at Kristen. His face very solemn, he answered, "I understand."

We left the others still hunting through the room for additional evidence and Kristen and I continued up to the end of the tunnel to the iron gate, just as Karen and I had done the previous day. We sat down close enough to the gate this time that direct sunlight from outside streamed down on us.

I was looking down at my shadow and Kristen's, not saying a word. Very softly in Karen's voice she said, "Yesterday I could not let the sun shine directly on me, Alex, and you never had the chance to see me in true sunlight. But, today, you can."

A chill ran down my back. I touched her face gently but I know my face must have shown the surprise I felt. "Karen ... Kristen ... I ... don't know what to say!"

She smiled and touched my face the way I'd touched hers, "Don't say anything, Alex! You don't have to say anything!"

My face wrought with frustration, I had to continue. "But I am so confused! Kristen, I'm not sure what to do! It was hard enough for me to allow myself to believe Karen loved me but, because I knew she would be gone in a few hours, I could understand the urgency of her ways." I touched her face again with the back of my hand and sighed. "But, with you, I know that, when we leave this house, you're not going to disappear forever! I just find it hard to accept that someone as beautiful as you would actually want to love someone as plain as me!"

A House

Her eyes pooled with tears and she tried to manage a smile. "I'm not sure how it happened, maybe just a coincidence, maybe because girls like Karen and I have similar problems, but, one night, in a dream, I was having a very bad time with a man who obviously wanted me for all the wrong reasons. I remember very clearly how terrible I felt because I knew I was being used and my heart was breaking." She laughed a humorless laugh. "The worst thing about the dream was how it paralleled my real daytime life! I was dating a man at the time, although not the man who was in the dream, and I felt like he might truly love me. But, in the back of my mind, I kept seeing little indications from him that he was more interested in the packaging than the contents."

She laid her head on my shoulder and held my hand, stroking the back of it as she continued. "During that dream a strange thing happened that had never happened before. A girl appeared. She was beautiful. Blonde—a perfect lady. And I knew in the dream that we were friends, although, in real life, I had never seen her before. But, in the dream, she knew me and I knew her and I knew she was the best friend I'd ever had. And, after the dream encounter with the guy who also vaguely appeared to be taking advantage of me, Karen and I had sat down and talked about men as though we were, in fact, two long time friends discussing a game plan on life itself."

She squeezed my hand. "Karen had told me that, all her life, she had experienced men just like the ones I'd experienced and she knew the reasons were the same as mine, the packaging rather than the contents. And then she mentioned one man that was different from the rest because he loved from the heart, not the eyes.

"From that night on, Karen appeared in most of my dreams and we spoke of love and heartbreak and men. And it was your name, your real name, that eventually came up. Karen had finally admitted that you were the man she had been talking about and you were also the man she had dreamed about when she was younger."

She snuggled even closer and lifted up enough to kiss my neck. "It was some time after that when she began to discuss her present condition with me and laid her history out for me to see. And it was then you began appearing in my dreams, after I pleaded with Karen to allow me to meet you."

She giggled. "I thought you were wonderful! What Karen had allowed me to see in my dreams I would guess was actually you in your real life! I thought you were a fine looking man and I came to love the way you treated those you worked with, especially the respect you showed the women. You had a way of making everyone feel comfortable being around you and, still, allowing the women to understand they were equals to their male counterparts and deserved every opportunity to prove it."

She adjusted her position. "And so I learned about you. And, after awhile, Karen actually brought you into my dreams and introduced us!"

I tried to look at her. "You're kidding!"

She giggled again. "No, I'm serious! I think Karen was able to 'borrow' you from your own dreams and actually bring you over into mine!"

She sat up and looked into my eyes. "Did you have any dreams about meeting women about a year ago

A House

where you were introduced to them and they skirted around the issues but, eventually, began making your acquaintance?"

I felt a little uncomfortable. "Well, yeah." I paused. "But I've had a lot of dreams about meeting women and trying to get to know them. I've always done that. It's my attempt to correct my lousy approach to them."

She smiled a shy smile and her voice was soft and coy. "I thought you were just fine! I thought you were always a perfect gentleman!"

My face frowned. "But being a perfect gentleman in my past never made me successful with women."

She laughed. "Yes, but the encounters in your real life were not as controlled as they were in our dreams!"

I didn't understand. "What do you mean?"

"Karen and I knew exactly what to do to uncover what kind of a man you were. And it had nothing to do with the conversation in the dreams! We'd bring in other situations and see how you reacted to them. We pretended to be employed in your secretarial staff. I posed as one rather plain, brown-haired girl with glasses and Karen posed as a dark-haired girl wearing braces on her teeth. You knew us in your dreams as Mary and Kathleen. We'd pretend to have man problems and, since you cared about us at work, you took great care at helping us understand how 'most' men treated women."

She laughed. "I'll never forget how you tried to give us hope, how you always tried to convince us that not all men were like the kind we'd described. Karen and I actually described men from our pasts and you, with your gentle heart, repeatedly attempted to reassure us that there were still some gentle, soft, caring men left."

I was embarrassed. I tried not to look directly into her eyes but stole a look at her anyway. Her look was tender and caring. She whispered. "You wouldn't look at us in the dream, either!" She stroked my face with the back of her fingers. "We both knew then and know now that you were talking about men … like <u>yourself</u>." Her eyes were pooled with tears. Softly she continued, "We knew, in fact, you were <u>talking about yourself!</u>"

I just sighed one big, uncomfortable sigh and nodded my head, still not wanting her to see the flush she had brought to my cheeks. She smiled and kissed my warm face.

"The best way to find out if someone is home is not always through the front door."

I tried to smile. "I think I understand."

"Good," she said. She continued, "So, once Karen and I had established what kind of man you were, we just sat back and watched you and, occasionally, brought you into my dreams to get to know you better."

I shook my head. "But why don't I remember any of this?"

She laughed so loud I could hear it echo down the tunnel. "It's because I didn't look like what I look like in real life! In your dreams I looked quite plain!"

I began to smile. "I think I remember now! Yes, I had a whole series of dreams where I grew very, very fond of a girl that was really nothing special to look at! But she had a heart of gold and I just couldn't help but want to be around her. She was always upset because she could not find a man who could love her for her

A House

heart. She was plain enough that I was not afraid of her." I paused and looked into her eyes, my cheeks still burning. Quietly I added, "Like I am … of you."

Kristen looked down at her feet and shyly answered, "Those fond feelings were actually for … me!" She paused and added, "And why should you be afraid of me?"

I sighed a big sigh. "I don't know. I've always been uncomfortable with attractive women."

She frowned like she was very upset by that. Quietly, she added, "But do you think you might be able to be comfortable with … this one?"

I tried to smile at her. I was so embarrassed I could hardly speak! My mouth was so dry I had difficulty just getting the words out of my throat. I had to clear my throat twice before the words would come out, my eyes were pooling with tears and I felt really, really bad all the way to the pit of my stomach. "I guess I could if she promised she wasn't just trying to make me feel better because we're together right at the moment."

The pools of tears that had welled in her eyes suddenly cascaded down her cheeks and she burst into some serious crying. She wrapped her arms around me and pulled herself as close as she could, her body jerking with the sobbing. But, through the tears she managed to say, "She just wants you to stay with her forever! She loves and needs you just the way you are!"

I held her like that forever. Eventually she stopped weeping and was able to part and look into my face. Her eyes swollen and red, her nose running and her lips trying to manage a smile, she said, "Alex, I really love you!"

I tried to make her feel better, like nothing had happened. I tried to smile and act like I was over being my shy, unpopular self. "And now I understand you so much better! I've actually known you for quite some time! I remember you asking me for advice pertaining to others." I paused. In a quiet voice I asked, "Were there really others?"

She shook her head. Shyly, she replied, "At first there were but, eventually, you were the 'others'."

I felt like I'd been set up. "So actually you were asking me how to deal with problems with others just to find out how I'd handle myself in the same situation?"

"Yes, that's right."

"And when you were telling me about problems in your life ... were the problems real?"

"Actually ... yes. I'd been dating different men and I came to ask you what you thought of them, from a man's point of view. You saw me as just a dear friend, just as you had with so many others, and you gave me advice from the heart." She made a little laugh. "I got the impression we'd become close friends and the attitude you gave me was one that implied you wanted nothing for me but the best things could be. I loved your expression about the difference between dating a man and having him as a friend. 'A man you're dating will tell you what you want to hear. A man that's really your friend will tell you what you don't want to hear.' And I understood and agreed."

A House

I squeezed her hand. "Well, that's true. That's how I have always been with all my dearest friends, male or female!"

She moved to put her arm behind me and hugged me closer. In almost a whisper she answered, "That's what I thought." She paused. "And that's what lets me love you so much."

We sat quietly for a few moments, letting everything settle in. Finally, she looked up at me. Quietly, she asked, "Does this mean ... you understand now?"

I nodded. In a whisper I answered, "I think so."

Again, we paused for an uncomfortable period. Again, very quietly, she asked, "Does this mean ... you might learn to ... love me?"

I looked at her. "Kristen, how could I help but love someone that has tried so hard to love <u>me?</u>"

We sat there, our shoulders touching, our hands holding one another, for a few more minutes while the others finished searching the room. Finally, they came out.

The chief spoke. "I think we have recovered as much out of that place as we're going to recover."

We stood up. "Good," I said. "Let's get out of here!"

By the time we got upstairs there was a team of people working over the evidence. The body of Elias Johnson had already been removed and the murder weapons were all gathered together in individual bags, ready for transporting out of the house.

The chief remarked, "Since the murder is only of historical significance, the town council and the mayor have asked if it would be all right to keep these artifacts as exhibits in the town's museum."

I nodded. "If there is no legal need for them, sir, I think it would be just fine."

However, Kristen corrected me. "Alex, we need some of those items over at my office today to complete some legal work left over from the original McNome will in order to close our business dealings with him."

I looked at her, and then at the chief. "That's right, chief. If we could just use the objects for a few hours I think it would be fine for you to keep them afterwards."

He smiled, the mayor smiled, and then the council members all smiled. "Agreed," he said. We all shook hands.

We all headed for the door with many additional officers all carrying items out as evidence. But, when the one officer carrying the toolbox with the knife and all the money in it got to the front door, he suddenly was struck by some unseen force and thrown backwards all the way to the staircase as a thundering shout echoed through the house.

The toolbox opened scattering the contents over the entire foyer. I then realized the officer had attempted something Mr. McNome had forbidden— he was attempting to leave the house with some of the McNome money!

We rushed to help the man and various group members scurried to retrieve the money and replace it in the toolbox. I apologized to the officer. "I thought, since the curse had been lifted, nothing like this would have happened!"

A House

The councilwoman, nearly scared to death, asked, "What exactly happened?"

I tried to explain. "Mr. McNome pledged no valuables would be taken from the house by anyone but the heir to the McNome estate!"

In terror she yelled, "But what about the rest of us?"

Quietly, I answered, "You should be ok." I looked toward the door. "Go ahead, Adam, try it."

He looked at me like I was crazy. I squinted my eyes as if to say, "What's the matter? Are you trying to scare these people to death?" He slowly walked toward the door and, finally, stepped through without incident. And then, one by one, the other members of our group all did the same until there was only Kristen and I left in the foyer.

Kristen handed me the toolbox and whispered. "Take this and walk through that doorway."

I looked at her like she'd asked me to take her place in front of a firing squad. But then, just as if she had, I'd resigned myself that it would be a far, far better thing to do than to let the same fate fall on her. So I started toward the door.

With each step I took I prepared myself for the impact I knew would hit at any second. I was a little uncomfortable by the additional fact that Kristen was always there right at my side, the entire way toward the door. But to my surprise, I was able to walk outside without incident!

I looked at Kristen. "But how?" I asked.

She whispered, "Only the heir to the estate could do that, remember?"

I nodded. "But what's that got to do with me?"

She looked at me like she'd been watching "Lifestyles of the Rich and Incredibly Stupid." She repeated. "Only the heir to the estate could do that, <u>Alex Jones!</u>"

I couldn't believe what I was hearing. Even when the mayor asked, "Does that mean ..." I didn't really answer because I really didn't believe it! But, at any rate, we packed all the things into the cars and prepared to head out to the law offices of Smith and Edwards.

I thanked the chief, his staff, and all the council members and swore we'd be in to see them all in a little while as soon as we handled some legal dealings in the law offices. They were all grinning from ear to ear and said they would all be waiting for us. As they all walked back to their cars, laughing and joking, I could hear them talking about arranging a celebration for the remainder of the day and evening. The chief was saying, "We'll get on the radio! We'll take our squad cars around the neighborhoods and broadcast the message! This is going to be <u>great</u>!"

Chapter 12
The Celebration

*W*e drove back to Kristen's office and entered, Adam and I plopping ourselves down on two chairs opposite her desk. She turned and opened a file cabinet with a large folder in it. With her back still toward us she spoke. "This is the file of the Jones family history. This starts back around 1880 with Brian McNome and his sister, Melissa, both living around New York City. Brian married and, around 1906, moved here with his wife, Sarah. However, his sister married Keith Jones and moved back to Ireland where, about 1902, they had a son, Ben."

She turned and placed the open file on her desk and continued to read. "But tragedy struck the Jones family about the same time it struck the McNome family. Around 1920 Ben had married Jessica McGee and they lived away from their family, it was rumored. As close as we could tell they'd moved to London, which didn't make his parents any too happy. Ben and his parents stopped speaking to each other and, even up until the time of their deaths in a ship accident, he never contacted them again. So, when the McNome family met with disaster, Ben not only did not know of it, he probably did not even know his uncle or his uncle's family!"

She turned a page. "Ben and Jessica moved back to the United States and had a son, Tom, who eventually married a young lady named Susan. They, in turn, had a son, Alex, and a daughter, Heather. But all members of the family but one were killed in a camping accident where three of the four were burned to death in a fire. All except …"

Weakly I answered, "Me."

Adam, looking skyward, figured, "That would make Brian McNome your … great-great uncle!"

Kristen smiled. "That's correct. And that also makes you the only living member of the McNome family."

Now I had some questions that needed answered. "But how did you find me?"

She laughed. "It wasn't as hard as discovering the rest of the family tree. After we knew who you were we went to the agency that placed you with the Williams family. The Williams were anxious to talk all about you, telling us where you were living, how successful you were, and how considerate you had been to them." She looked up from the papers and smiled her little all-knowing smile. "They were so anxious to tell me what a great son you were. Your adopted mom wanted me to know how generous and considerate you had been to them in your success, even though, throughout your childhood, there was little they could do for you to help."

I couldn't look her in the eyes. "They were the only parents I'd ever known. They did everything they could for me all my life to make me what I am today." I finally tried to look up at her. "Wouldn't you have tried making things up to them for the sacrifices they made while you were growing up?"

A House

Kristen's face softened. "Many would not. You did. That's what makes a difference."

I shook my head. "If it hadn't been for being able to take that toolbox from the house I would say this was all fabricated just to pin it on somebody. But, seeing as how the house itself is convinced I'm the right person, what else can I say?"

She nodded. "And that was why I wanted you to do that, even though doing it in front of others was not exactly what I'd had on my mind. But, you must admit, it was pretty convincing!"

Adam just leaned back in his chair. "Oh, boy!" was all he could say.

I sighed. "So, what do we do now?"

She got up from behind her desk. "Well, the first thing we have to do is assemble all the artifacts we needed to gather and lift the curse from the McNome family!"

Adam stirred. "Do you mean it's not over yet?"

She was walking out toward the cars. "No, not really. We have to bring all the artifacts here, next to the will, and say something that will forever remove the doubt and shame from the McNome family and release them from their curse."

We all went out to the cars and retrieved the items and headed back to the office. There, with the will, we put everything in a pile, including the diary, the missing pages, and the murder weapons. We all held hands to form a circle and lowered our heads and closed our eyes. Without any prompting from any of us, Adam spoke. "Here we gather 'round the clues, the McNome family's paid its dues. The tools of death from dust be sifted, the lifetime curse, at last, has lifted." A cold wind, like a miniature tornado, swept across the desktop and began blowing papers and objects all over the room. We opened our eyes just in time to see a bright green glow emanating from the center of the circle we formed with our arms as the items began rotating on the desk and moving into the air.

The wind became so severe we could no longer keep our eyes fully open and Kristen yelled above the noise of the wind, "Keep holding hands until this is all over!" It continued for another minute, the knife shooting off the desk and past the heads of Adam and I and embedding itself in a distant bookcase, other implements just scattering to the wind like so many strands of straw. And then, with a thundering boom, the room darkened and the wind died and everything returned to normal.

The room was as quiet as death itself and none of us said a word. Until Kristen looked into my eyes and said, in Karen's voice, "Thank you Adam, Alex. Thank you for freeing us forever."

She moved close to me and hugged me as she always had before, completing it with a kiss on my neck. In a whisper next to my ear she said, "Kristen is free of me now, Alex, but please do not forget me. I will be with her but she will not feel it, nor will you. But don't forget me. I will still be waiting for you to join me, and I will enjoy you and I and Kristen and Alex to forever be together in this place I now see ahead of me."

I began to weep. "Karen, I love you. Please don't leave me again."

A House

The whisper was accompanied with warm tears on my neck. "I cannot stay as I am. I must go. But I will always love you—you know that. For now, love Kristen as you love me and I will know how much you care. I carefully brought you both together to love each other all the days of your lives because I love you both so much I could not bear to see you be lonely for the many years yet to pass before we will all be together."

I held her tight to me and she held on to me as well. And then, in a few seconds, Kristen went limp and I was holding an unconscious woman in my arms.

I picked her up and headed over to a couch in the far end of the room. I laid her down on the couch and just began to ask Adam to find something to bring her back around when she began to revive.

She knew nothing of what had happened while Karen had been talking but she still knew who I was and she remembered everything that had happened in the house. I chanced asking, "Do you remember anything about Karen McNome?"

Weakly she smiled, her eyes still mostly shut, and she whispered, "Yes, I remember Karen. I love Karen. She's my best friend."

And then her eyes opened wide. She didn't say anything for a moment and then she stated in a monotone, "Karen's gone."

I stroked her forehead with the back of my hand. "Yes, yes, I know. But are you all right?"

Her face softened again. Quietly, she answered, "Yes, I'm fine."

I hesitated to ask. Whispering, I continued, "And do you ... still love me?"

G. Voyten

A loving look covered her face. She took my head in her hands and brought it down to her face and kissed me softly. When we parted she said, "Yes, yes, I still love you! Of <u>course</u> I still love you!"

In a few moments she sat up on the couch and I sat down beside her, holding her hand. We both felt dejected about losing Karen forever. I sighed. "Well, what do we do now?"

Looking off into the distance she answered, "I guess we just go on living, the way Karen and I had dreamed so many times."

I stood up. "I guess we could begin by taking these things back to the town hall and turning them over to those people over there."

Kristen stood as though nothing had happened. "Yes! And they swore up and down that, if you were successful at clearing up that mess at the mansion, they were going to declare a town celebration!"

She went to her phone. "I'll call over there and tell them we're on our way over!"

After her phone call we gathered the items from the desk and from around the room and began putting them in the trunk of her car. Without even thinking about it I put Karen's diary back in my jacket pocket where it had been before. We then all got into Kristen's car and she drove us back to the town hall where we were met by hundreds of screaming townspeople cheering and dancing as a marching band played. The mayor came out and made a speech. "This day means much to the people of Jefferson Junction. We have had to live with sixty years of guilt over a needless violent act that our forefathers did nothing to avoid or solve. Today, in the company of a brave team

A House

of investigators, we thank them for finally lifting the curse from the McNome mansion, as well as the curse on Jefferson Junction."

He turned to me and handed me a small box with a golden key in it. "As the duly appointed representative of the Township of Jefferson Junction, I hereby present you and your brave friend with the key to the city and declare this day to forever after be known as 'Brian McNome Day'."

The crowd broke into screams and shouts of excitement and approval. The marching band broke into a marching song. We turned over the items to the mayor and, for each item handed over, the town cheered. But I kept the diary. I never wanted to allow the diary out of my possession.

As though by some kind of miracle, the town had changed from the sleepy little township into a pulsing, exciting city. Vendors of foods and items seemed to come out of the woodwork. Bands set up all around the town square and music could be heard of a dozen flavors, all playing at the same time. Merchants opened their doors and volunteered gifts to Adam and I. Families set up picnic tables and began giving away about every kind of food imaginable. The generosity and friendship pouring from the members of the township was like nothing I had ever experience in all my days in the city! I felt like I was home!

It was very enjoyable.

There were news reporters from not only the town paper but from wire services as well. One asked me what was the first thing I wanted to do, now that it was all over.

I became very serious. "The first thing I'd like to do is bury those people who died in that house. They were fine people who lived a very good, clean, respectable life and they deserve to be treated with respect now."

For a moment, the crowd became very serious. Faces sobered and heads nodded. The muttering in the crowd agreed that, in the morning, the McNome family and the other two lives that perished in that house would be laid to rest in a proper manner. To return the mood of the celebration I added, "And then I would like to discuss with the city fathers what I can do to help further develop the community and enhance its prosperity!"

The entire crowd cheered and screamed and the celebration restarted with more energy than ever before! Dozens of people came up to me to shake my hand, women hugged me, men patted my back. The bands broke out in marching songs again.

Throughout the celebrating, Kristen held on to me, in one way or another, everywhere we went. No matter whom I spoke with, where I went, or what I did, I kept volleying fond glances between Kristen and myself. The longer time went on, the better I felt about everything.

One of the things that stood out strongest in my mind was talk of my new money, or, better said, the lack of it! Seeing how I was now the owner of a mansion and great wealth, I would have expected at least one crass individual to ask about my plans for the money and the impact it might have on the township. But, to a man, not one comment. To the contrary, the comments all concerned what they could do to help me

A House

fix up the house and make things right with the family and the town again.

I looked at Adam. Sitting there with a smug look on his face, he began to nod his head. "I agree with you, Alex, we've got to stay here."

Kristen's eyes lit up. "Do you mean ... you're both going to move here?"

I nodded, smiling ear to ear. "I think I can manage my businesses from here just as well as anywhere. Besides, I have all this mess to clear up here."

She bounced up and down like a child, her eyes as wide as saucers. "Yes! That's right! And you haven't even heard the good news yet about what you've inherited!"

I looked at her with a confused look on my face. "You mean there's more to all this?"

She raised her head and laughed a hearty laugh. "Of course there's more!" She laughed so much tears formed in the corners of her eyes. "Alex! You've inherited a fortune! Just because Brian McNome died didn't mean his empire died with him! There has been sixty years of progress in his industries! His bank accounts have multiplied themselves over hundreds of times! Alex, you've inherited over a billion dollars in cash and liquid assets!"

Adam nearly fell from his chair! I sat stunned! I thought for a moment. "I guess deciding what to do around here has a whole new meaning now!"

She giggled and squeezed me. "I guess it'll take a little longer to figure out what you're going to do when you grow up than it would have before!"

Adam laughed. "Boy is that an understatement!"

The celebrating was still going on around us, people occasionally stopping by to congratulate us in conquering the house, but, as the evening wore on, we were left more and more to ourselves. And that was a good thing as well. I wanted more information from Kristen about the state of the township and the county. I wanted to figure out what we had to do, if anything, to improve the lifestyles of those in the community.

"The village is like most small towns. It neither prospers nor dies, it just makes it on what it has."

"If they were able to do something that they feel could improve things here, what do you think the majority would say?"

She thought about it for a moment. "That's hard to say. It might be a better question to bring up with the town council."

I pressed the issue. "Any guesses?"

"They probably would want more commercial business and less industrial. There are quite a few small towns in this area and no major shopping facilities. Most area residents must drive far away to do things city people take for granted, like going to a motion picture or a shopping mall."

I nodded. "I think I understand."

The evening was winding to a close for Adam and I. The townspeople were still celebrating but Adam and I had gotten very little rest over the period of the last day and night. It was approaching 1:30 in the morning and I thought of an important thing: Verifying that, in fact, the curse on the house had been lifted!

I thought Adam and Kristen were going to laugh at me when I suggested going back to the house and seeing if the reenactment of Brian McNome's death

A House

took place at 2:00. They didn't laugh. They didn't even smile. They looked worried and shocked. "Look, guys, how do we know if everything worked? No, I'd feel much better going back and verifying nothing happens." I paused. "Besides, if the house is actually mine, and, if I'm ever going to live in it, I'd like to verify it's livable."

Still not smiling, we all got back in Kristen's car, drove back to her house, picked up my car, and took the short drive back to the house. The gate was still wide open, the house glowed in the moonlight, and we drove this time right up in front of the house and prepared to enter once again.

Chapter 13
The Final Battle

*T*he porch floorboards complained again this time just as they had the previous day, the front door, still not locked, allowed us to enter, and the house, as dark as death itself, seemed to be waiting for us to return.

We sat on the bottom steps to the staircase going to the second floor and waited for two o'clock to arrive. When it did, there was no reenactment of Brian McNome's death, or anyone's death, for that matter, but something was still there, still waiting for us. Some forces were still at work in the house!

Adam spoke at exactly two o'clock. In the softest whisper he said, "We're not alone in this room right now. I can feel the presence of at least three others, not of this earth."

The only light in the room was a storm lamp I'd placed halfway between us and the doorway at the front of the house. The lamp, though, supplied enough light to the foyer that we could have made out the presence of additional beings, earthly or otherwise. However, at that very moment, the lamp began to dim and the room began to darken. Kristen grew more and more frightened and I could feel the circulation in my one arm diminishing as she gripped it tighter with every fleeting moment.

The moaning returned to the room and dark objects began to appear in the corners. The objects approached

A House

us, very, very slowly, and grew in size until, by the time they were within reach, they were human sized.

We stood as they arrived before us. The low moaning, luckily, never got much louder than just a whisper but it still had the ability to unnerve us all, just as it had always done before.

One dark object formed arms, legs, and a head. Even in the darkness I could make out the appearance of a man, although it was like looking at someone trapped within a dark, translucent covering. The hand reached out toward me, very slowly, and not at all menacingly. At the same time, I extended my hand as well, as if to allow this entity to touch my hand. And, in an instant, it did!

But the strangest of all things happened at that very instant! At the point where our fingers touched the black finger turned white! The whiteness began climbing up the hand and arm and down the entire body until, in a matter of seconds, the entire entity had changed from black to white! When the face turned white I could clearly make out the features, watching the transformation happening to itself, it began to smile.

The man then looked into my eyes. It spoke in a whisper so low I could barely hear it. "Brian McNome told us to seek you out and you would not fear us. Sarah McNome told us you were good and would help us fight the evil that cursed us to this existence. Karen McNome told us you could help us go to our final rest if we would but let you."

The image of a man smiled at me. "You came back. Your drive to help overcame your fear of the unexplainable and unknown. You knew our souls were eternally cursed to unrest and that we were enslaved with the powers of evil and yet you returned to free us from our bonds."

The image began moving away, toward the back door, still not touching the floor, still smiling. In a voice louder now but not at all threatening, he spoke as his image faded from view. "Your goodness and bravery have freed me to go to my eternal rest, a cleansed soul no longer cursed with the chains of evil. I will be eternally grateful …"

As he faded away three other blackened shapes all approached. One by one, they all touched my hand. One by one, they all turned white and faded into the room. And the moaning had all but disappeared.

I thought everything was over until Adam detected one more soul headed our way "This one is even more powerful, Alex. This one is … *evil itself*." The room darkened more than ever before and the moaning increased. I could barely make out Adam's face but what I could make out was near terror. "This one is death. This one is violence. This one has taken the lives of others." He stared into my eyes with a look that could stop time itself. ***"This one knows us!"***

The moaning grew very strong, the air intensified, there was a static feel to everything. The walls began hissing like foam from an angry ocean and a foul stench grew in the room.

Coming down the hallway from the library was a huge black shape hovering about three feet above the ground. The feeling in the air made breathing difficult and Kristen took one look at the object and screamed as loud as she could.

A House

She didn't know whether to run or hang on me but she attempted to bolt for the front door. A thunderous rumble echoed through the room as the front door slammed shut and a flash of lightening broke the darkness of the room. Kristen's body went sailing backward through the air and landed with skidding sounds at my feet.

Adam and I bent down to pick Kristen up but she was completely unconscious. Instead we dragged her over to the steps and laid her down there.

The black object approached us and the intensity in the room grew. The walls appeared to be bleeding and the carpet on the stairs seemed to be alive and conforming to our shapes, trying to hold us where we stood.

The black object then began to take on the shape of a human and, even in the darkness, I thought I knew who it would be. Without hesitation, I spoke out in a loud, confident voice. "I'm not surprised to see you here, Elias. I'm sorry you have been cursed to this house but I felt earlier today that the chance your soul would be condemned to roam these halls was very strong."

Elias was angry with us and he would not approach the way the others had. Instead, he hovered many feet above us near the large chandelier. In a voice very young, very loud, and very angry, he answered. "I knew you would come back. I knew you would not escape me." Even in the dark I could see his dark, young features smiling a cruel smile at me.

He laughed a horrible, evil laugh and the house itself shook with it, the sound reverberating through every fiber of the structure. Again, in a voice loud and confident, he spoke as his shape approached us. "I killed the McNome family and I will finish the job with you!"

His huge shape grew closer and closer as the moaning and hissing increased. Adam fell to the stairs and screamed for his life. I looked over at him for only an instant and saw him lying on the steps, unconscious. I fell backwards and felt something bulky in my jacket pocket and remembered what it was: Karen McNome's diary!

I hastily reached for it as Elias was putting his black hands around my throat. The pressure from his large, icy hands immediately began squeezing and I instantly stopped breathing! I continued to struggle, momentarily forgetting about the diary and only attempting to remove those cold hands of steel from my windpipe but it was like trying to move air! I thought I was going to die!

My vision began blacking out and I was losing all strength in my arms before I finally remembered the diary once more. In a last second struggle for life itself I frantically reached back into my jacket pocket and found the diary! With my last ounce of strength I thrust the diary at his heart.

Screams from a dozen voices screamed so loud I thought I'd never hear again as lightening flashed and thunder boomed and the house itself seemed to retract in horror and pain. The image of Elias immediately soared skyward, grabbing at it's chest and screaming in a bone shattering frequency and turned from black to gray but grew larger and larger in size, as though it were a balloon inflating past its normal capacity. And then, at the height of the screaming and thunder and

A House

lightening, the image blasted apart in a thousand pieces with a blinding light and a cavernous noise that echoed around the house for many seconds afterwards!

The house grew silent. The light from the lamp returned to normal. The storm outside, real or otherwise, was instantly gone. Adam lay on the steps, barely breathing, holding his throat with one hand and his chest with the other. Kristen was just about to regain consciousness. But the house was silent. The house did not feel possessed. I could feel myself passing out.

The next thing I knew Adam was standing over me trying to wipe my face with a wet cloth, where he'd found it I could not begin to guess. I felt soft hands holding my head on either side and then realized my head was resting on … Kristen's lap!

Weakly she asked, "What happened?"

I tried to smile back. Very weakly and barely loud enough to hear I answered, "You just had a memorable minute with Elias Johnson's evil ghost."

She shuddered. "And?"

I swallowed dryly. I noticed I was having a very difficult time swallowing at all. "I don't feel his presence in the air anymore." I looked over at Adam. "Adam? Do you feel anything else is here besides us now?"

He stopped screwing around with the wet cloth on my head. He began looking around, his eyes strangely not focusing. His stares were high in the room, looking off into deep darkness. As though not truly believing it for himself he said, "It's incredible! I don't feel the presence of anything else here now!"

He kept looking around, over and over, as though he expected things to change. "No, I still don't feel any other presence in this house except our own."

We paused a moment. Kristen asked one final time. "This is your last chance, Adam. Is there something left here or not?"

He looked at us with a look of utter amazement. "No! Nothing! The three Civil War buddies and our close acquaintance, Elias, are all gone! Vanished! Forever!"

I breathlessly wheezed. "Forever. 'Nothing is forever.'"

Kristen replied, "Don't talk like that, Alex!"

We gathered ourselves and collected the few things we'd brought with us and headed back outside to the car. We climbed in and I looked over at Kristen, a confused look on my face. "Ok, it's nearly three in the morning. What do we do about someplace to stay?"

Adam laughed. "We could unload our stuff and stay here for the night!"

I yawned back at him. "Well, that would be good enough for me." I looked at Kristen "But what about you?"

She grinned. She grinned a very long time and didn't say a word. Finally she said, "Gee ... would you mind if we did?"

We all laughed. 'No, I wouldn't mind! After all, we must get used to it sometime!"

So we got sleeping gear from the trunk of my car and headed back into the house. The night was warm, the moon was still shining brightly, and, in the moonlight, the house looked beautiful.

A House

When we got back to the front door I put down my gear and picked Kristen up and carried her through the doorway. She nearly fought me. "Hey! I thought you were only supposed to do that if you were married!"

I snickered. "A mere technicality."

She stopped struggling. "Do you mean …?"

I smiled at her. "Can we arrange it in the morning?"

She grinned ear to ear and hugged me and kissed me. Breathlessly, she answered, "<u>Yes</u>!"

Adam carried my gear and we all headed up the stairs, me still carrying Kristen. No, she wasn't such a big girl that she made a load too big to carry up the steps. And she hugged and kissed me the whole way up the stairs nearly causing me to lose my balance twice!

When we got to the top of the stairs Adam started back to the rooms we had occupied the night before and then paused and looked back at me. In a low voice he said, "Oh, I'm sorry. I just assumed we'd use the same rooms we'd used last night." He paused, possibly waiting for a response but then continued before getting one. "Was I right?"

I looked at Kristen and then back at him. "Yes, I think that would be a good idea."

Adam continued on to the room he'd had the previous night saying back over his shoulder, "That's good because I've already got this one broken in the way I like it."

I smiled. Looking at Kristen I added, "And I have very fond memories of the one I spent the night in as well." She looked at me with a shy, knowing look on her face and I carried her into the room with me.

She whispered, "Do you think it's proper for us to share a room for the night with your friend knowing what we're doing?"

I chuckled a little. "To tell you the truth, it doesn't matter to me!" I paused. "Does it matter to you?"

She giggled. "No, I guess not!"

I put her on the bed and went back to Adam and got the rest of my gear. By the time I'd returned to the room Kristen had the bed cleaned off and made up for sleeping. Still whispering she said, "Why do I feel like I've gone through this before?"

I laughed. "Why, indeed!"

The smile on her face left. The look turned to one of deep affection and love. She walked slowly over to me and threw her arms around my neck. She kissed me softly, squeezing herself closer to me. I let my arms wrap around her and our bodies molded to each other.

We sat on the edge of the bed, just as Karen and I had done the previous night. Again, I didn't feel like I should be doing what I was doing because, after all, it was only a few hours ago that I had met this beautiful young woman and I didn't feel I had any right to be intimate with her. So, I thought, putting sexual thoughts away somewhere to concentrate on emotional and social issues would probably be the best plan to follow.

We propped ourselves up on the bed with just the bedside candle burning on the nightstand next to the bed and one over on the vanity on the far end of the room next to Karen's photograph which we both just sat and stared at. Kristen moved close to me and our arms wound around each other so we were close as we

A House

sat there, our minds probably racing off in opposite directions.

And then, quietly, Kristen asked, "What are you thinking about right at this moment?"

I hesitated. "I don't think you really want to know."

She squeezed me. "Yes I do. Really, now, tell me." She hesitated. "Is it sex?" she said under her breath.

"Actually ... not!" I thought I was about to insult her but she asked, didn't she? "Actually I was thinking about ... Karen."

She repositioned herself on the bed again. "Well, yes, I was thinking about Karen, too, but ... what else?"

I sighed. "Well, I was just thinking about how quickly everything happened with her. I was trying to piece things together in my mind about her and ... about you."

She moved closer again, her head coming to rest on my shoulder, her lips near my ear. She whispered, "Well, tell me the part you were thinking about me."

I pulled her closer and kissed her forehead. "I'm still trying to figure things out. You've got to understand I've never been too good with women in intimate situations."

"But I know you have. You were discussing intimate things with me in the dreams we shared."

"Yes, but that's different. It's always easy to love someone enough to be their brother and suggest solutions to daily problems between them and someone else." I paused awkwardly. More quietly I added, "It's a little more difficult to be the object of their problems!"

She sighed. "I'm not sure I completely understand."

I continued. "I've always loved my closest female friends on an affectionate level, always nurturing them, making them feel comfortable, knowing what to say to help them with their real lives. But, when push came to shove, the problems were always between them and someone else. Not ever did they consider me as the object of their deepest love, only of their affections and, at that, only second to someone else they cared for more."

"Oh, I think I understand now. You're trying to say that, in all the years of giving advice, you never got involved enough with a woman to be the first object of both her love and affection, but only something less."

I nodded. "Yes, that's right. I have had countless women love me in my life, kiss me, hug me, hold me, cherish me. But they always went off with someone else and remembered me as the nice guy that helped them get their head straight. Nobody ever wanted me for all time, only for the time they needed support of their fragile feelings."

"But what about your feelings? Did they ever consider that?"

"In a word ... no," I said very quietly.

She laid against me very quietly for a long time, so long I thought she'd fallen asleep But that would have been ok, I told myself. Having her fall asleep would have meant she would stop the questioning that was only succeeding in making me feel miserable anyway. But then she spoke again. In a voice as soft as face powder she said, "Alex, I love you." She paused. "And I love you first and best and always."

A House

She sat up so she could face me. "Alex, believe me, you are the most important man in my life and have been for a long time." Tears were pouring from her green eyes. "I don't want you to think I just want to use you or have you as my casual friend to help me through life when I might possibly devote my true love and affection to another man! Alex! You <u>are</u> the other man!"

She dove at me and wrapped herself just as tight as she could to me and wept a big boo-hoo kind of cry. I could feel the tears soaking into my chest and I didn't exactly know what to do except hold on to her and pull her closer to me.

Finally, in a whisper, I attempted to say something to try to make things better. I felt my chances were zip, but I thought I'd try as best I could. "Kristen, please, don't cry over me! Ok?" Talk about a stupid thing to say! I knew it sounded stupid even to me! How could it possibly make her feel better? But I never claimed to be good with my own problems, only with those of others!

She wouldn't raise her head from my chest but tried to talk anyway. "Just hold me. Alex. I need you so much tonight. I need to know you're not going to leave me just because you don't feel you have a chance with me!"

I held tightly to her and stroked her hair. "It'll be all right, really. Just calm yourself down! And we can talk this out, just like in the dreams, ok?"

She squeezed me and sobbed, "Ok."

She took a few minutes to calm herself down and we began a conversation to try getting to know each other better. I felt the only way we'd have a chance was to sit and have many, many intimate talks about what we felt toward the world, other people, each other, and ourselves. Throwing in talk about Karen occasionally wouldn't hurt, I assured myself. I knew Kristen had felt much of the relationship I'd gone through with Karen so it could serve as a common frame of reference.

"When I was a young man I had absolutely terrible luck with people, not just women, mind you, but people. There were all these little groups that you had to be like in order to be accepted by them and I'd decided by the time I was thirteen that never again would I change who I was or how I acted just to be accepted by some group of people. And I carried that philosophy with me the rest of my life. So groups came and went, people came and went, and I stayed the same.

"We all grew up and they had to keep changing to match the group they wanted to be accepted by. I didn't change. I still felt that the best thing I could be to myself was to be myself, care if I wanted to care, laugh if I wanted to laugh, cry if I wanted to cry, love if I wanted to love. I felt, if there were people in the world that happened to like the way I was, then the group I'd belong to would be my group, not a group thought up by somebody else.

"And so, all my life, I have been accepted by the kindest, most loving people in any group of people, the kind of people that appreciate caring about each other. But, my only undoing, my shyness, kept any woman from ever taking me more serious than to allow me to be affectionately loved. When it came to something more permanent and deep, there was always someone

A House

else willing to say what needed to be said or do what needed to be done in order to win the woman, no matter if what was said or done was the truth. And I would not do that. I would never lie to someone I loved. Often as not, I could not even bring myself to express my true feelings. And that is why I was never loved back as much as I loved." I paused. Quietly, I added, "Wouldn't you find it difficult to love a man that had such a difficult time telling you how he felt that you came to doubt his feelings altogether?"

Kristen sat up and her red, swollen, tearful eyes looked deep into mine. In a voice as soft as rain she said only, "But you are now. You are telling me your feelings!"

I sighed. "Yes, at least I'm trying to tell you how I feel."

She paused a moment and then continued. "But you never really said how you feel about me."

I squeezed her. "How could I resist loving you? Like Karen, how could I possibly resist loving a woman that has seen through my inability to express my feelings properly and still love me?" I kissed her gently. "Of course I love you! I love you more than anything that has ever entered my life! You, and Karen, have shown me there are women in the world that can care about me as much as I care back! You must be and must always remain to be the most important two people I have ever known or will ever know."

She rose up and looked at me through her red, swollen eyes, beaming a smile from ear to ear. Gently she answered, "That's exactly what I've been waiting to hear! Alex! You did it! You were finally able to express yourself!"

Kristen moved her entire body up higher in the bed so our faces were next to each other. She softly brought her face closer, closer, until she was kissing me.

We kissed very tenderly. And then, as though a replay of the night before, Kristen took the lead. "Alex, I want you to love me as much as I love you and as much as you felt you loved Karen." She paused. Questioning, she added, "Do you think that's possible?"

I stroked her hair and answered, "Kristen, all I need from you is to know you will love me, really love me, for more than just now. I know that sounds like something the woman should be saying, but I'm not just interested in entertainment. I want someone that gets the greatest satisfaction just being together and doing exactly what we're doing, whether things go farther or not."

She smiled a sly smile. "That's funny. That would have been what I would have said to any other man!" She giggled. "And I think the approach I was preparing to take would, somehow, sound like the approach most men would have taken to 'get what they came after'!"

I smiled. "But you don't have to make an approach with me. All I need from you, especially tonight, is you. We don't have to push our relationship to the limits. I've told every woman I've ever known I would never do anything to them they did not want to do. And, obviously, none ever wanted to do very much!"

A House

The sly look came back to her face as she smiled at me. In a whisper she said, "But what if one of them wanted more?"

I grinned. "Then I would have taken that into consideration under the circumstances at hand."

"And what about the circumstances at hand tonight?"

I looked at her. "I'm not really sure what the circumstances are tonight."

She kissed me. "The circumstances are that you're in an old, abandoned house, locked in a room with a woman that has told you repeatedly how much she loves you who is laying on top of you, putting her leg between yours, and is telling you you can do the kind of thing you would normally want to do with a woman that you love as much as you love this one."

I pulled her closer to me. In a whisper I answered, "I would say, under conditions like that, and seeing how I love that woman as much as I do, I would probably want to do exactly the same thing I did last night under conditions that were almost identical!"

She sat up to her knees and began taking off her silk blouse. When it was undone she unfastened her short leather skirt and slid it off her legs, all the while staring deep into my eyes. Wearing her remaining clothing she laid back on top of me again, hugged and kissed me very sensuously, and asked me what I thought. I only said I thought she was headed in the right direction as I squeezed her closer to me and ran my hands up and down the back of her body.

She kissed me passionately and I let my hands run over her. She then got back to her knees and removed the remainder of her clothing, one piece at a time, incredibly slowly. Finally, as she began undoing mine as well, she whispered, "I think we both understand which direction circumstances are going to carry us tonight, don't we?"

As I finished removing my clothes, I whispered back, "I think so."

She climbed under the covers with me, our bare skin burning against each other, our hands searching over each other's body, our lips pressing hard against one another, and nature followed its own course once again.

Chapter 14
A Final Tribute

*A*fter what had to be remembered as one of the most memorable times in my life, the next thing I knew it was morning again and Kristen and I were still naked in bed together, arms tightly wrapped around each other. Sunlight was streaming in through the open curtains of the room and my mind thought of Karen and Kristen and tried to understand how all this had happened.

My mind drifted in a little while to thoughts of what would happen next. No, not just thoughts of the morning and getting organized and cleaning the house and burying the McNomes, but thoughts of where was my future to head. What would become of Kristen and Adam and me?

The house was quiet— so quiet even making some sounds didn't seem to make much sound. I silently, carefully, pulled away from Kristen and put on my clothes. I felt Karen's diary in my pocket and I decided to sit and read it while I was waiting for Adam and Kristen to finally wake.

The diary was about the last two years of Karen's brief life. It was filled with stories that she had already summarized with me, stories of school and Mary and such. But then, about a month before her death, before any of the robberies began, she started talking about her ... dreams. And I sat there with chills running down my back, time after time, reading encounters with a man in her dreams ... a man named ... Alex Williams!

Alex Williams had become to Karen what Karen had become to me: A beacon of hope in a world of futility. Her descriptions of his build, his look, his mannerisms, were mine. He helped her solve her emotional problems, face her courtship shortcomings, just as I would have done had she been a contemporary friend of mine! In all, her Alex Williams was a perfect picture of what I felt I was!

Page after page I read of this girl's dreams of this man, a man she came to love more than any real man she had ever met. Page after page of lines praying for the day this man would actually come to her and love her like she wanted so desperately to be loved.

Tears ran down my cheeks as I continued reading. Sometimes I cried so hard I had to stop reading because my eyes could not see the words on the page and I didn't want my tears to obliterate the ink. But the woman in the book represented the woman I had always wanted to find ... and finally had. My heart broke as I continued to read of how terribly the men of her time treated her and how, luckily, she always had her problems helped by her dream man, Alex Williams. No wonder Alex Williams meant so much to her. He was the only man she could trust!

I came to understand, as well, that the problems she had experienced were quite similar to those I had encountered in my own life. She had basically been a "good girl," always considerate of the needs of others. She was rich and that was different from me in my early days, but her wealth was kept from her and the

A House

little money she had in her younger days she freely shared with others. And the overpowering theme in all her writings was the futility of finding someone who could love her, really love her, for what she was inside. Her fantasy was to meet a man in the darkness, similar to a confessional, and get to know him without ever seeing each other. That way, she assured herself, she would know the man loved her for how she was, not what she was.

She admitted to herself the shortcomings of her ways. No, it would not be easy to find someone who truly loved her because she had not discovered a way of separating her looks and her station from her heart. She dreamed of the day, though, that she would find a way of doing just that.

She also literally created the dialogue for her courtships from those she'd had in her dreams … with me. It appeared she had many conversations with "me" where I advised her about what points in a personality were important to explore to assure the intentions of the other person. And, in her dreams, she learned the only man she had met to satisfy those qualifications was the man in her dreams who had stated them! Why? Because, she felt, the man in her dreams understood, in his own mind, that he would never be anything more to her than a dear, personal friend, and never a lover. She asked him why. He said because no woman before had ever let him mean enough in her heart to let it be so. She stated about that dream that, if she ever met that man in real life, she would force him to understand that she loved him more than anything else in her life because he had always managed to put her needs before his own and, according to his own words which she lived by from that time on, that was what one should expect from someone who truly loved you.

I looked outside and watched the sun rise above the trees across the street and listened to the wind gently blowing against the house, tears still streaming down my cheeks. And suddenly, silently, warm hands were behind me, rubbing my shoulders. A soft voice consoled me. "Don't weep for her, Alex. You gave her in one evening everything she ever wanted in her life. You not only gave her short life the meaning she had always searched for, but you reinforced her dreams of you where you were her best friend and confidant."

I wiped my eyes and turned around. Kristen was wearing a silk nightgown from Karen's closet, as beautiful as the day it was put there, and she was as beautiful as any woman could have been in it.

I put my arms around her waist and pulled my head to her stomach and cried. Kristen's arms wrapped behind me and pulled me closer to her, a kiss was planted on top my head. She whispered, "And now, the best thing you can do for Karen, the best thing you can do for me, the best thing you can do for yourself, is to let me love you as she loved you."

I squeezed her tightly to me. "I will. I promise I will."

We stayed like that for a little while, Kristen just stroking the top of my head, me just squeezing tighter to her, and then we parted and she got dressed.

I watched her closely as she put her clothes back on. Incredible to think that she loved me, I kept thinking over and over. I still could not comprehend how a woman could learn to love me without ever physically meeting me and how it could be probably

A House

one of the most beautiful women in the world. Not only was her face stunning but also her body was perfectly proportioned. Her look was so perfect it was difficult not dwelling on the outside image and remembering what a perfect person lived within.

We were both completely dressed and unlocked the door and headed down the hall. Before we even got to the stairway Adam poked his head from his room and sleepily remarked, "Hey, you guys. Can't you wait for the happy-go-lucky sidekick character?"

We laughed and waited and I answered, "C'mon, 'Gabby'!" Then we all went down to the first floor. We didn't hesitate but went directly outside to the car. "I don't know about you two but I want somewhere where I can have a good breakfast and then a bathroom where I can scrape this hair from my face, shower, and climb into some fresh clothes," I said, scratching my two-day old beard stubble.

Everyone in the car with seat belts fastened, Kristen remarked, "Well, head down toward the center of town and I'll take you to my place where you can both clean up while I whip us up a super breakfast. Does 'Eggs Benedict' sound good?"

Adam hollered, "Sound good? After living on dust bunnies and old spider webs for two days I could probably eat the shells!"

It was just a matter of minutes before we were pulling up in front of a beautiful contemporary two-story home on the outskirts of town. Home, Kristen assured me. "I live her by myself, even though it has four bedrooms and gobs of space. But I like the space and don't mind the isolation." She looked at us and smiled. "And you both are more than welcome to live here while the mansion is being renovated."

We piled out of the car and into the house. I noticed the home had not been locked. Why? Kristen answered, "Because there's no need here. We've never had a robbery in this town in all the years I've lived here, and that's all my life."

Adam and I took the bags we'd grabbed from the trunk and each headed to a separate bathroom and simultaneously began cleaning up for breakfast. Kristen busied herself in the kitchen making coffee and the rest of the food fare.

I had a lot on my mind as I was cleaning myself up. As I looked in the mirror to shave I noticed I still had black marks on my neck from the hands of Elias Johnson. As I put the razor to my neck I whispered to myself, "I just hope those are just bruises and aren't going to be a permanent fixture on my neck!"

The shower felt wonderful. My body felt like it had fallen down a cliff and been picked up by trash haulers to be taken to the hospital for minor repairs. The warm water pulsed over my muscles and took some of the knots out of the rigging for me.

I'd brought in a fresh set of clothing and, in a few more minutes, I was fresh and ready to face the day. Well, I thought, I wasn't ever going to look better, but, at least, I'd be clean!

I headed out to the kitchen where Adam and Kristen were already sitting down to begin eating. I sighed. "It seems like the mess over at the McNome mansion was just a bad dream now."

A House

Adam nodded. "I can remember how terrifying parts of it were but it still doesn't feel like it actually happened!"

Kristen smiled. "But if it hadn't happened, we'd never be sitting here together!"

Breakfast finished, dishes cleaned up, Kristen began making phone calls. She arranged for the burial of the bodies from the house, she talked to the mayor, she talked to the chief of police, and she arranged for a council meeting between me, her, and them. And she added, "Alex, I don't want you to leave this town any too soon." She paused. Her head and voice lowered. "I don't want to lose you."

I stroked her face. Gently, I answered, "You're never going to lose me now! Just try to!"

She rushed to my arms and shared a big hug with me. I added, for I felt I should, "And there was one important phone call you forgot. Something about … marriage?"

She stepped back, her eyes pooled with tears. As though she were surprised she said, "You mean you weren't kidding?"

I laughed. "Of <u>course</u> not! Would I fool around about something as serious as that?"

Her eyes burst into tears and she started laughing. She ran to the phone, began to dial, put it down, ran back to me, gave me a hug and then a kiss, and then ran back to the phone and began to arrange things for a wedding. She laughed again. "I don't really have any friends from out of town to invite!" She laughed another time. "I don't ever have very many friends from in town to invite!" And then she paused. In a more reserved voice she added quietly, "Do you?"

I laughed. "Hey! I carry my best friend with me! 'Alex Express: Don't leave home without him'!"

We decided on an order. We wanted to be married first and have the funeral afterwards. Kristen thought Karen would like to see that things had worked out before being laid to her final rest. I agreed.

And that was how the day worked out. We did what we had to do to become legally married before two in the afternoon, we had arranged to bury Brian, Sarah, and Karen McNome in a plot that had been bought by them seventy years before, we had arranged to bury the mysterious vagrant man, and, under more restrained circumstances, we had arranged for the burial of Elias Johnson in a lonely area of another cemetery far removed from the town where his curse had lasted sixty years.

Our wedding was small, rushed, and exciting! In just the few hours since we'd gotten up, Kristen had arranged blood tests, the marriage license (having friends at city hall helped!), the location, the minister, and personally invited all her friends by telephone who canceled what they were doing and rushed over to the little chapel where we met to be wed.

Of course, representing my side of the family was … Adam. There was no time to fly my adopted parents in but I did telephone them to tell them about it. Kristen's side was better represented with dozens of people, all grinning, all happy, all so glad Kristen had finally met the man she had dreamed of meeting. None of them, however, knew she had actually dreamed of meeting him!

We had agreed to have a reception in the evening, after all the business of the day was over, and we had

A House

contacted the biggest hall in town—the town hall—for the celebration. The mayor insisted the only way of assuring all townspeople were invited, according to my wishes, was to make the announcement on the local radio station! And so he did!

It appeared the entire town had turned out for the burial of the McNome family. Many hundreds of people crowded around during the ceremony. I was surprised to see how many people cried during the ceremony, as though they had personally known the family. Kristen whispered, "The town has always felt it was, somehow, responsible for some part of the problems that happened to the McNome family. It is relieving sixty years of guilt here today."

I nodded my head as the coffins were placed in the crypt with the "McNome" name engraved on it nearly a century before.

I whispered back to Kristen, "Now I guess a debt has been repaid by both the community and by me."

Tears pooled in my eyes and Kristen wept as Karen's coffin was rolled into the crypt. We followed behind and watched as the coffins were all placed within stone containers inside the little block building, the stone lids placed down over them.

Kristen reached over and put a single red rose on Karen's grave. She whispered, "Good bye, my special friend," as we turned to walk out into the bright light of day and in front of the crowd still standing there.

We received the people, one by one, as they extended their sympathies to us. Few said more than that but some added a welcome to the community and vowed to help make things better for the McNome family by helping with the restoration of the family name and estate to where it belonged. I thanked them each warmly and sincerely. Those who offered their help I welcomed to my new home for whatever reason they saw fit.

After our McNome ceremony was over we attended a small group at the grave of the vagrant being buried on the other side of the cemetery. This man, his family unknown, had no mourners other than the three of us and the crew responsible for his burial. On his headstone I had the stonecutter inscribe: "May this lonely friend rest in peace forever." The date of death only read the year of the deaths of the McNome's, since I didn't know exactly when the man had met his fate and there was no year of birth.

We all got in my car and traveled to another cemetery in another town to witness the burial of Elias Johnson. Kristen had helped me choose one where I could have a large stone cross placed as a headstone in such a way that the shadow, year 'round, would always cast down across the grave. This was the remains of a soul still cursed and I didn't want to chance it rising again and killing us in our sleep.

Our trip back to Jefferson Junction ahead of us, the three of us began considering what the future would bring us. I figured we should make a game plan because I didn't want to face losing either of my dearest friends, my new wife or my old companion. And so I attempted to make a pact with them.

"The future will be bright for us. We'll bring the township back to where it wants to be, we'll renovate the mansion and move back into it and explore all its hidden places, and we'll consolidate all the business interests under one plan. Of course, the law firm of

A House

Smith and Edwards should continue to represent all the McNome interests. Who better to run businesses than those that have done so for over sixty years? And Adam will continue to be ever vigil and ever close." I looked at him. "You find a house around here you want and it's yours, if it's for sale, my friend. Or I'll build you whatever you want."

Kristen laughed. "For that matter, I can give him mine. I have a mansion to move into now!"

I added, "And, at least in the short term, of course, I'll need you close to us, Adam, to help us solve all the other mysteries of the house."

He questioned, looking a little unsure about my statement. "Short term?"

I looked over at him. "Adam, I can't force you to rip up your life and move out here permanently unless you want to."

"But, what would you prefer to have me do?" he asked.

"Well, personally, I'd like you to be here with Kris and I forever! <u>Adam</u>! You're still my best friend and always will be!"

He chuckled. "Well, I guess the two of you have settled my future for me already!"

Kristen looked at each of us, holding our upper arms. "And I've got two of the best friends anyone could ever hope to find. And I owe it all to a lady that died sixty years ago." A tear ran down her cheek. "May we be happy together forever."

Adam and I chimed in together, "Forever."

About The Author

*D*rawing on personal psychic experiences in his past, this author has written murder mysteries revolving around a fictitious house, family, and town in Virginia. Trying to incorporate many personal events witnessed in his past, the ghostly transitions will seem hauntingly familiar to many that have also experienced similar events. The author designed the house inside and out to accurately portray the look and hidden passages described throughout the novels. A computer database specialist by trade, he finds writing fiction a welcome relief from the details of computer science. The author is the father of three, and his children also have the ability to see things others can't see, and they frequently gather to discuss their experiences.

Printed in the United States
65552LVS00001B